NORTH POLE UNLIMITED COLLECTION 4

NOEL AND MERRILY, JACK AND BELLE

ELLE RUSH

SBD ENTERTAINMENT

Formatted with Vellum

This book is dedicated to the one I love. Thanks, Ross, for supporting my love for all things Christmas.

NOEL AND MERRILY

A North Pole Unlimited Sweet Christmas Romance
by
Elle Rush

BLURB

Struggling singer Merrily Sweet has five days and five thousand kilometres to figure out her life. As she drives across Canada, she must either find the inspiration to write some new songs or decide to abandon her musical career entirely. Then she gets an emergency call. She can't leave fellow North Pole Unlimited employee Noel stranded over the holidays, so now she has company on her road trip.

IT whiz Noel Sprouse loves the holidays, but he's not ready to launch the Santa-based app he created. When he finds himself stuck on the wrong coast after an airport incident, his only chance to make it home for Christmas is as a passenger with a former teen pop sensation who becomes obsessed with his genius idea.

With Noel providing the inspiration and Merrily supplying the encouragement, can these two road-trippers get everything they want for the holidays – success, romance, and home in time for Christmas dinner?

PROLOGUE

North Pole Unlimited Headquarters
December, Manitoba

Nick Klassen, vice-president of Human Resources at North Pole Unlimited and terrible present wrapper, set a massive box in the middle of his desk. The difficulty wasn't in the size or the weight of the package. The problem was that his lovely wife snooped and spied on her presents, and he had to find a safe place to wrap her just-delivered Christmas gift before she sniffed it out like she had the previous year. And the year before that. All that he needed now was a full roll of tape, a tube of wrapping paper, and some music to set the mood.

"New Songs for an Old-Fashioned Christmas" began playing quietly on his phone in the background. Soon he was out of tape and was hunched over, digging in a drawer for more when his desk phone rang. He didn't officially start work until eight o'clock, but this close to the holidays, every call could be an emergency. "North Pole Unlimited. Human Resources. Nick Klassen speaking."

"Hi, Nick, uh, Mr. Klassen, sir. It's Noel. Noel Sprouse. I'm trying to reach someone who can reschedule a flight home for me, but nobody in the travel department is answering their phones or responding to emails. Can you help me?" The man with the deep voice on the other end of the line sounded frazzled from what Nick could hear over the background noise.

A nebulous picture of a slightly-younger-than-him, dark-haired man formed in his head. "Noel? Where are you?" As far as he knew, Noel Sprouse was due to start his shift in the Information Technology department in half an hour; he shouldn't be stuck in an airport on company business during the busiest time of the year.

"Vancouver. I was at a conference."

Nick nodded to himself, trying to shake the pre-coffee cobwebs loose. Now he remembered. "The Global Digital Marketing Experience conference. Dave Block sent you as his replacement after he broke his leg," he recalled. "Did you miss your flight home? Jilly is going to have something to say if she has to book you another flight back to Winnipeg the week before Christmas." Nobody liked it when Jilly Lewis-Fredericks, his executive assistant, started to rant, but Noel was relatively new to the company and might not know better yet.

"No, Mr. Klassen, I didn't miss it. It's six o'clock here now, and my Air Canada flight was scheduled for seven-oh-five," Noel said.

"Just Nick is fine. Did you oversleep and now you can't get to the airport in time?"

"I'm *at* the airport," Noel clarified. "They've shut down the entire Domestic Departures terminal. There was some kind of fire. Sprinklers have gone off and the fire department is on scene. I was here at five, and it was already a disaster area. They aren't letting anybody through the doors."

"Oh!" That was an entirely different kettle of fish. Jilly refused to reward incompetence, but this was anything but Noel's own fault. "Can you find some place nearby to wait it out for a while? Jilly's not in yet, but I'll get back to you as quickly as I can with a new itinerary."

"Thanks, Mr. Klas—Nick. I'm flying out of Winnipeg on the twenty-second. I haven't made it back to Montreal for the last two Christmases and my mom will kill me if I miss another one."

"Hang tight, Noel. I'll call you back soon."

Nick could go through Jilly's desk and find the log-in codes to get into the various travel portals and start looking for a flight to get Noel home. But as the VP of HR, Nick prided himself on knowing all the employees and associates working for North Pole Unlimited. There might be someone in the vicinity who could offer a more direct hand. He was scrolling through potential allies in the area when his executive assistant arrived.

"You're at work early, boss."

"Good thing, too. Noel Sprouse is stranded in Vancouver. There's been an incident at the airport and his flight is cancelled. I'm trying to find an alternative way to get him home."

Jilly groaned, and one of her brown eyes started twitching. "It's going to be a nightmare finding a flight at this late date this close to Christmas."

"That's what I said," Nick agreed. "Especially out of Vancouver. I thought it might be easier to find one if he was departing from Calgary."

Jilly hummed as she waited for the travel site to load. "It would give us more options. How is he supposed to get there though?"

The song on his phone changed to "I'll Be Home For Christmas", and it reminded him of an upcoming appointment in his calendar. "We have someone driving from Vancouver to Calgary today. Noel could potentially catch a lift."

That caught her attention. "Who?"

When he spoke the name, Jilly began to giggle, then laugh in earnest.

"What?" he asked.

"You have no idea what you've done, do you?"

CHAPTER 1

DECEMBER 20TH
Vancouver, British Columbia

The Christmas season on the west coast of British Columbia was a brand-new experience for Merrily Sweet. Growing up in Ontario meant that December was all about toques and mittens and wet snow, not golfing in a light jacket or strings of red bulbs hung on still-green trees. It was novel and weird, but she'd miss it.

She pulled out her phone and took a selfie with the Pacific Ocean in the background to mark the start of her trip. ***Good-bye Vancouver. Heading east for a white Christmas. #Roadtripping #5000KM.*** Merrily posted it to her various social media accounts and slipped her phone back into her pocket. As gorgeous as the scenery was, she was looking forward to being home for the holidays. She threw her parka on the back seat, looked at the crashing waves one more time, and climbed into her bright yellow van—lovingly referred to as the Lemon Mobile—to start her trek to Ottawa.

Vancouver had been a good layover city to earn a few dollars at the end of her summer tour. Her seasonal concert schedule had been a little sparser than last year, which had been worse than the year before that. Merry Sweet was a teenaged popstar who had been on her way out by the time she turned twenty-two. Then Merrily had been officially dropped by her music label at twenty-five and now, at twenty-eight, she was doing community concerts, filling school gymnasiums in small towns across the country.

She'd ended her tour in central BC and made her way to Vancouver to visit friends and pick up some studio work. She did a few radio ads, sang back-up for a couple up-and-coming bands, and tried her hand at narrating an audio book. It paid the bills, but the work was nothing to write home about.

Speaking of writing, or rather not speaking of it, she refused to look at the notebook in the bag beside her. She hadn't written anything in months. Merrily couldn't remember the last time she'd cracked one of her music books to play around with new lyrics. She'd been on a treadmill of singing covers and her old hits, although lately she'd been doing Christmas concerts wherever she could get a booking at a seniors' residence or holiday party. She needed some heartfelt inspiration. Or at the very least some new scenery to get her creative juices flowing.

Somehow, she didn't think she'd find that inspiration on her cell phone, but it was the season for miracles. Merrily read the text again, frowned in confusion, and called the sender directly for clarification. "Hi, Nick. I got your text. Yes, I'm still planning on driving home to Ottawa from the west coast. I'm literally sitting in my car ready to leave. How did you know and why are you asking?"

She'd thought it was an innocent question at the time. The next thing she knew, she was being thoroughly flattered by her self-proclaimed number one fan and had agreed to do him a teeny-tiny favour.

"We're desperate, and you're there," Nick Klassen had said. "Noel is one of North Pole Unlimited's best IT guys. He was in Vancouver for a conference and was ready to fly home today when there was a fire at the airport."

"I heard about that. All outgoing flights cancelled." The radio was calling it a holiday disaster, and Merrily couldn't argue with the description.

"We managed to rebook him on a flight tomorrow morning out of Calgary, but I need to get him there. You mentioned in one of our meetings that you're driving through there on your way home. Can you please, please give him a lift? I guarantee he'll be a complete gentleman."

A thousand kilometres through the mountains with a stranger in the passenger seat. It sounded delightful. On the other hand, Nick Klassen had personally contacted her on behalf North Pole Unlimited and hired her to sing three songs on their annual Christmas CD. That contract had saved her bacon when her summer tour had ended. She owed him. "It's ten hours of driving through the Rockies. I'll do my best, but I can't promise to get him there on time. That depends on weather and luck."

"He'll take it," Nick had said.

Half an hour later she pulled up to the front doors of

the Longfellow Vancouver Hotel, waiting for her new travel buddy to appear. As Merrily waited to enter the long circular hotel driveway, she returned the wave of a cheerful, hunched, salt-and-pepper-haired man who was driving a classic, blue pick-up truck with a stocking hanging from its antenna which that was exiting the same drive. She pulled in the loading zone behind three taxis and was about to text Nick that she'd arrived, when she spotted her target heading towards her. The tall man with the goatee and curly brown hair matched the company photo that Jilly had sent her, but the image didn't do him any justice. "I don't believe it. It's Noel *Freaking* Sprouse," she said to herself.

The rookie stock car racer had been in the news at the same time she'd been climbing the charts, although more of the stories about Noel "Fast Times" Sprouse were about his daredevil exploits off the track rather than on. If she recalled correctly, his racing career had ended with a second-place win in a race that would have taken him to the next level, followed by getting smacked by an empty school bus during a thunderstorm. Merrily didn't know how the former driver had ended up in Information Technology but it seemed like they'd both found themselves working for North Pole Unlimited in one role or another.

She rolled down the window and waved.

He nodded and picked up his pace. When he crouched to look through the open window, his jaw dropped open. "What? You're Merry Sweet!"

Yeah, this trip was going to be a blast. She loved to be called by an old nickname that reminded her of her fizzled musical career.

Her face must have expressed that perfectly. "I'm sorry. I had a poster of you up in my room when I was a tecnager." Noel winced and tried again. "That's probably not much better. How about we start this conversation over?" he asked. "Hi, my name is Noel Sprouse. If you're the Ms. Sweet that Nick Klassen sent, I am very glad to meet you and I'm incredibly grateful for the ride."

She cautiously took the olive branch he offered. "I am the Merrily Sweet that Nick sent. It's nice to meet you, Noel. Do you have any other luggage to bring out?" When he hoisted a computer bag in one hand and a carry-on in the other, she pointed behind her. "I'm good to go if you are. I made a space for your stuff. Hop in, it's a thousand kilometres to Calgary."

An hour and one pit stop at a donut shop later, they finally passed the last neighbourhood of the Greater Vancouver Area and headed east into the mountains. The silence stretched fragilely between them. "That was a bit of a rough start. I was only ever Merry on stage. Not even my family calls me that. It wasn't my favourite nickname when I was topping the charts. Now it's more of a direct line to a bad memory. If we can stick to plain Merrily, I'd appreciate it."

Noel nodded in understanding. Although he wasn't quite as tall as she first thought, it had only taken him five minutes in the Lemon Mobile to toss his jacket into the back and push the seat back as far as it could to give himself much needed leg room. "I hear that. A lot of people look at me and still see Fast Times Sprouse. But that was a lifetime ago—one I'm trying to leave in the dust. After I stopped racing, I went back to school and got my computer sciences degree. I've worked for North Pole

Unlimited for almost a year now, but my history makes it easy for folks to jump to conclusions about me."

Merrily snuck a look at him. "I have to confess that I had pictures of you, too. My uncles were all gearheads, so we spent a lot of time at the local speedways. Let's call it even. Tell me what exactly you do for North Pole Unlimited. Have you ever met Jilly Lewis-Fredericks? What's she's like in person, because she's scarily efficient."

Noel laughed, then relaxed into the passenger seat for the first time. "She's terrifying."

CHAPTER 2

Noel took a sip of his now-cool coffee and tried not to stare. He was in a car with Merrily *Freaking* Sweet. She looked different than her album covers, with her bright pink hair and hockey sweater instead of the old image he had of her as a blonde in a mini dress. He'd still recognize her anywhere. Merrily and her music had been unavoidable in his formative years; he hadn't followed the pop princess for her catchy tunes, but her videos had been fun and great eye-candy. Like a lot of teenaged sensations, she'd faded from public life after a few songs. He hadn't thought of her in years except when he heard one of her songs on the radio.

"What about you? How did you end up involved as a North Pole Unlimited associate?" he asked. The company had partner companies around the world. Working in the IT department meant Noel got to speak with a lot of them online as they communicated with head office. They had florists, bakeries, and games manufacturers but he couldn't figure out how a singer would fit into the corporate structure.

"They put out a new holiday album every couple of years. This year I contributed three songs to it. I did it all remotely, but I promised Nick Klassen that I'd stop by in person the next time I drove through Manitoba."

He suddenly wanted to hear that album. "What songs did you do?"

She briefly looked at him, a huge grin on her face, before she returned her attention to the twisty, inclining road. "In a weird but relevant twist of fate, I sang my favourite Christmas carol of all time. 'I'll Be Home For Christmas.' And here you are."

Noel laughed with her. "I approve of that choice. Although it's not my favourite."

"What is your favourite?"

"Grandma Got Run Over By a Reindeer."

"Another classic," she said with a laugh. Merrily went quiet for a couple minutes as a convoy of semi-trucks passed them going in the other direction. Noel had a ton of driving experience, but none of it was in the mountains. He appreciated her caution, but he'd still prefer to be the one behind the wheel. "Do you like Christmas carols?" Merrily asked hesitantly.

"Absolutely. I love Christmas. Carols were a constant in my house. Thankfully my mom didn't play them twenty-four hours a day for weeks on end, so we didn't get sick of them. They were a constant background for meals and presents and family nights in December. My aunt and her wife are the same way whenever we visit at the holidays."

"Would you mind if I put some on? Reception isn't great for the next six hours or so, so I loaded my phone with a few playlists, and one is Christmas songs. The high-altitude snow after all the green in Vancouver is putting me in the holiday spirit," she said.

Honestly, all the green had freaked Noel out a little, too. "Go for it."

They made pleasant chitchat, and he watched the scenery until they pulled into Kamloops four hours later. Merrily's Christmas playlist had ended three hours earlier, and he had offered an hour of classic heavy metal, which had been followed by some current top forty.

But what Noel absolutely loved was that he—occasionally, barely audibly—heard Merrily singing along when she liked a song. He hadn't found any pattern to the music that triggered her, but he felt like he'd had a private concert for most of the drive.

Unfortunately, she caught his grin at a red light, and stopped in the middle of a word. "I was doing it again, wasn't I?"

"I don't mind."

"I'm still sorry. I only do it in the car and I don't have many passengers, so most people don't know I'm a singalong addict," she continued to apologize. "But I think it's only fair that if you know one of my secrets, I should know one of yours. What have you got, Noel Sprouse, that isn't harmful but that nobody else knows about?"

He didn't think that her love of music was anything to be embarrassed about. He understood a passion that overrode everything else, and, as it stood, music was relatively harmless. Noel waited until they had their subs and were eating at a picnic table outside the restaurant before he answered. "I created a Christmas app. I started working on it just before I got my degree. While I was at the conference, I figured out the final tweaks I need to make before I can release it."

"That's cool. It sounds like a lot of work. What kind of app is it?"

Noel paused. He hadn't told a soul about this. Mostly because it wasn't something he should be working on.

After he retired from racing, he didn't know what to do with himself. He'd gone through a string of interviews that his father had arranged, much to his dad's frustration. They'd had more than one argument about Noel's inability to commit to a new job. After he'd lost out on position number three, he realized that his dad had been right. Noel had buckled down to find something else he was interested in and had settled on website construction, but even after a year in school and getting his degree, his family was still certain he was going to abandon it for yet another new opportunity.

He'd won the North Pole Unlimited internship through hard work and good luck. When they'd offered him a job at the end of the term, Noel had jumped on the chance. And he loved what he did. But he did have a shiny idea in his back pocket that he picked away at in his personal time.

The problem was that if he told his bosses that he had created a holiday app, he was afraid questions would start about when he'd had time to work on it. Noel had been hired to do website maintenance. If they, like his family, thought he couldn't stay focused on his assigned job for six months, he was doomed.

"I'm calling it 'Christmas Every Day'. You are assigned a daily task to keep the Christmas spirit alive throughout the year." Noel grimaced; it sounded silly when he said it out loud. It had originally started as a calendar he was putting together for his mom and aunts, but he'd decided it would be fun to experiment with it.

Hundreds of hours later, he had over six hundred Christmas activities stored on his phone tied to his digital calendar.

"I love that idea. What would today's activity be?"

Noel knew December weighed heavily into community-oriented tasks. He called up December twentieth and read it. "Do a favor for a stranger."

Merrily laughed. "I already did that one. Can you tell me another one?"

He pulled up a random month and read the task for August third. "Look at an old Christmas photo, and text hello to the person in it."

She nodded. "Good one." Merrily pulled up her photos and scrolled for a while. "This is perfect!" she said, turning the screen to face him. It showed her in a Santa hat brandishing a wrapping paper tube at another young woman who was fending her off with a bag of ribbons and a stuffed reindeer. "That's Ash. She was my hair, make-up, and wardrobe wrangler on my last studio album tour. I hear she's working on the Mercer Brothers tour now." She quickly attached the photo to a text. "Saw this and thought of you. Hope you are 'wrapping' things up on tour so you can have a relaxing Christmas. XO Merrily." She hit send then looked up. "It's been way too long since I said hi to her. That was a good idea."

"You don't think it's too juvenile?"

"Did you see me in that picture? Juvenile isn't an issue."

The second leg of their trip was all downhill. They took a quick stretch break at Salmon Arm, then pushed through to Banff, where they took a twilight walking break at the iconic Banff Springs Hotel to look at the lights and decorations. After that, they got hot chocolates to go for the final hour's drive out of the Rockies into Calgary.

Merrily pulled up to the entrance of the airport hotel twelve hours after she picked him up. "Thanks for your company today. It made driving through the mountains a little easier."

They were saying goodbye much too soon. Noel couldn't remember the last time he'd spent so long in close quarters with a stranger and thought their time together had ended too quickly. He'd met singers and actors while he'd had his time in the limelight. Most of them hadn't impressed him; Merrily had. She was funny, gorgeous, easy to talk to, and had great taste in music that thankfully extended beyond pop. He couldn't have asked for more. Plus, she was unbelievably generous. "Thank you again for the ride. Because of you, I can get home tomorrow, catch my flight on Wednesday, and make it home to Montreal for Christmas. It's going to mean the world to my family for me to be home this year."

"You're very welcome. Good luck with the rest of your trip. And with your app. Let me know when it goes on the market."

That wouldn't be happening any time soon, but it was nice to have some positive feedback from the first person who had ever seen it. "Thanks. I'll do that." He had saved her contact information knowing he'd never have a chance to use it again. Now maybe, someday, he'd have the chance.

Noel checked in to his hotel, checked into his flight, and checked out a bunch of old Merrily Sweet videos until he fell asleep.

CHAPTER 3

As much as Merrily wanted to fill up on waffles and maple syrup, she forced herself to have a more balanced, nutritious breakfast for the road. One egg over easy, a fruit cup, two slices of bacon, and a single slice of rye bread, heavily buttered. She'd find a donut shop on the road for a mid-morning sugar bump. She had another thousand kilometres to drive today. Thankfully, it was all a straight shot on flat, prairie highways, which would be good since she hadn't had a terrific sleep.

After her long day with Noel, and his confession about his secret app, she'd been inspired to pull out an old music notebook. Nothing romantic had come of their time together, but a day's worth of uninterrupted male company–and handsome, intelligent, entertaining company at that–had sparked something inside her. She'd hoped that spark would translate into something on the page.

Merrily was shocked to see that the last entry had been dated a year ago, a few months after she'd struck out with the last agent she'd contacted before she'd decided to go it alone. But with Noel on her mind, she'd given it a try. After half a dozen false starts, she'd shoved the notebook back into her bag in disgust. The desire was there, but her talent had abandoned her.

Merrily raised her head and stuck out her chin. She had four thousand kilometres to go. She could rediscover her mojo at any point along that highway.

After paying her breakfast bill, she tapped her weather app to ensure she still had the blue skies the weather station had promise the night before. While she was verifying that no blizzards were brewing along her route, her phone buzzed in her hand.

It was Noel. *Are you still in Calgary?*

Checked out but still in hotel restaurant for an early start. Aren't you supposed to be in the air?

Moose on the runway. They destroyed a pick-up truck that tried to scare them off. Debris all over the runway. Half the flights are delayed. Other half cancelled. Guess which group I'm in.

Merrily's jaw dropped. The fact that a moose had taken out a truck wasn't surprising. Those half-ton beasts always had the right of way. It was the fact that an entire herd had made it onto a runway. They weren't going to leave until they wanted to. All those poor, stranded people! *What are you going to do?*

See if my favourite driver ever thinks she can be at the Winnipeg airport before two pm tomorrow and if she has room for a passenger? PLEASE?!?!

Merrily heard the desperation without the inter-robangs. *No chance Nick or Jilly can rebook you through to Montreal?*

Not 2 days before Christmas. Nothing's available.

She was already heading in that direction, so it wasn't like Noel would be an additional expense. It would mean an earlier start than she wanted the next morning to get him to the Winnipeg airport on time, but it wasn't terribly inconvenient. *Be outside your hotel in ten minutes. First snacks are on you.*

Forget snacks, you're getting chocolates and roses. You rock! Three tiny dots appeared and disappeared. *That was only a music joke if you liked it.*

She grinned. *Nine minutes. And we have to make a stop before we leave town.*

Noel was ready and waiting. He was wearing the charcoal cargo pants, a change from his dress pants the day before, and a Calgary sweatshirt peaked out from his open jacket. He didn't immediately take it off, shivering from his short dash through the freezing loading zone.

His seat was still in position, so he didn't have to adjust it to give himself extra leg room. "Brr, that's a wicked wind. Also, good morning and thank you again. You're a real Christmas angel, Merrily. What errand do you have to run before we head out?"

"I have special request from Nick Klassen. I need grab a Christmas present for him."

"The VP of Human Resources asked you for a personal favour?"

"He's my number one fan, and he's the one who approached me with the Christmas album contract. I could hardly say no." Merrily shrugged. "He said it's packaged and paid for. All I have to do is pick it up. He even texted directions."

Noel programmed his next playlist as she followed her GPS to their next stop. They pulled up to a bustling parking lot in front of a glass-fronted storefront. Totally Iced Bakery was doing brisk business. She hoped the errand wouldn't take too long.

It didn't. The pair of women behind the counter kept the line moving, and every few minutes a young man would bring a fresh tray from the back to restock the display cases. When it was their turn to order, a brown paper bag with red ribbons wrapped around the handles and "JILLY" in big black letters printed on the side caught Merrily's eye. "What can I get you?" the peppy Black woman with the bright pink lipstick asked.

Merrily pointed. "That, I think. Nick Klassen from December sent me to pick something up, but he didn't say what. I'm supposed to ask for Kris?"

"I'm Kris Singleton and this is my bakery. Nick said you'd be coming." The flour-dusted woman grabbed the package to pass it over but held onto the handles even once Merrily had a firm grip. Her brown eyes opened wide, and Merrily braced, knowing what was coming.

"You're... You're..."

"Merrily Sweet. Nice to meet you, Kris." This was the fun part of the job.

"Yeah, you're Merry Sweet. And you're in my bakery! I used to listen to your stuff all the time. I mean, I still like it—"

That reminder was the less fun part. "I'm glad you enjoyed it. Thanks for having this ready for us. We're driving back to Winnipeg today, and Nick sounded desperate."

"Oh, he is." Kris hesitated. "Would it be totally out of line to ask if I could get a selfie with you? Rudy will die of jealousy. I can bribe you with cookies if that would help."

"I'll pay for the bribe, but yes to the cookies, please. Those look amazing." A photo of Kris, Noel, and her displaying a huge open box of goodies soon appeared on her profile. ***Pit stop in Calgary for Totally Iced Christmas cookies #Shortbread4Ever #road-tripping #NoelSprouseNavigatorExtraordinaire.***

After a second round of photos, they were finally on their way. The Lemon Mobile had just cleared the city limits and was heading east on the Trans-Canada highway when Merrily's curiosity overcame her. "What would today's Christmas Every Day's activity be?"

When she'd checked into her hotel the night before, she found a return text from Ashleigh with another photo of them and a short update of her friend's life, including news that she was now engaged. Merrily had responded with congratulations. She never would have known if Noel hadn't have given her the nudge.

He ducked his head, and the shy gesture was adorably cute. "Well?" she prompted.

"Spot a vehicle sporting a Christmas decoration."

"That sounds like fun. I'll keep my eyes peeled. We have another thousand kilometres today. I'm planning to stop in Virden, just over the Manitoba border, for the night. Winnipeg is almost four hours past that, but I don't want to push my luck. With an early start, I can have you at the Winnipeg airport before noon. Will that work?" she asked.

Driving cross-country—across almost the entire country—had been a deliberate choice. Merrily had wanted alone time to come to some decisions about what she was going to do with her future. Her summer tour had provided one definitive answer: it didn't pay to be a concert musician if she didn't have anything new to offer her fans. Her time in Vancouver taught her that she could make a living doing studio work, while her single foray into being an audio book narrator gave her another path to consider. But if she wanted to be the same kind of professional musician she'd been at the beginning of her career, she had to make new music. Last night had been a shocking kick in the pants when she'd tried and failed utterly.

After she dropped off Noel in Winnipeg, she would have another twenty-five hundred kilometres to figure the rest of her life out. There was nothing like adding life-changing decisions to the stress of the Christmas holidays.

She needed to work on her timing.

Having Noel in the passenger seat was postponing her self-reflection, but Merrily didn't mind. It gave her an opportunity to get the questions she needed to ask herself straight in her head. Plus, Noel was cute and funny and filling the tank at every other gas station. She could have worse company on a drive. She didn't know anyone else who would compile a playlist to compete with her Christmas carol selection, but Noel had put one together. It was short with only a dozen songs, but one of them was completely new to her and two were versions of songs by artists she didn't recognize.

As they headed towards rolling pin country, Merrily cranked the volume and music filled the van. "Flat land, here we come!"

Moose Jaw, Saskatchewan, was not a vital pit stop. They didn't need gas or food or a bathroom break. Merrily just wanted to stop for a freezing cold selfie with an old friend: Mac the Moose, a thirty-four-foot moose statue on the edge of the city.

"I can't believe you're making me do this," Noel said, teeth chattering as he took a picture of her at a distance to get more of the massive, three-storey-tall moose in the frame.

"If Canadians don't appreciate their own roadside attractions, who else will?" Merrily countered. "Besides, it's a ten-metre-tall moose. How often do you see that?"

"How often have you seen it?" Noel countered.

"Five times."

"Do you take a selfie with him every time?"

"Of course. After meeting him the first time, it would be rude if I didn't visit when I was in town," she said as she typed. ***Hello to an old friend #MacTheMoose #HelloMooseJaw #Roadtripping.***

Noel was lucky this was the only statue he was going to have to stop at during their time together. Merrily had an album full of photos of roadside attractions, including Mac in all the seasons. She also had one of Flintabbatey Flonatin from her trip to Flin Flon, Manitoba, two years earlier, and several of Tyra, the world's largest dinosaur in Drumheller. If they hadn't been a hurry, she might have made a loop north-east of Calgary and then turned south-east to visit her gigantic, green buddy. The stops were the best parts of road trips. She couldn't believe Noel didn't know that.

"When I was driving, the point was to make it to the finish line as quickly as possible," he explained. "Detours

were strongly discouraged and resulted in disquali-
fication."

"What's the fun in that?" she'd asked.

He was laughing too hard to answer.

An hour past Regina, with two more hours of
Saskatchewan prairie to go, Noel shocked her when he
said, "You haven't sung along to a playlist or the radio all
day. You can, you know. It doesn't bother me. I like the
private concert."

"I'm not feeling the music today," she admitted.

"Is it the company?"

"No!" She didn't want him feeling bad for the rest of
the trip. "After driving through the mountains, I was
feeling inspired from the scenery, so I tried to write something. It did not go well." She snickered ruefully. "It
sounded like a Grandma June's Chicken commercial."

"I never liked her tenders anyway," Noel said loyally.
"What's today's scenery doing for you?"

There were many things that could be said about the
province they were currently crossing. "Saskatchewan:
easy to draw, hard to spell" was a common one. Flat was
another. There were endless fields of farmland, currently
barren and snow-covered, stretching as far as the eye
could see. But it had beauty in its own way when the sun
shone out of the clear blue sky and the snow sparkled
liked diamonds on the ground. "It's okay."

But the scenery wasn't what was inspiring her as she
concentrated on the dashed line on the blacktop in front
of her. She was too busy trying not to get distracted by the
man beside her, who kept making her laugh and was so
focused on getting them to their destination. Merrily had
an active dating life, but it had been ages since she'd hit it
off with somebody so completely. If they'd met at a party

and not through work, she'd absolutely date Noel if he asked. But he was depending on her for a ride, and he wasn't going to jeopardize that even if he wanted to, which he hadn't indicated at all.

Unless and until he did, she'd enjoy Noel as an excellent travelling companion. Unfortunately, she couldn't come up with a way to work his good vibes and their road trip energy into a song. Her brain was jumping from Christmas songs to rock tunes to ballads, but nothing was sticking.

Not that it mattered. She didn't have a recording company to write for. Still, the whole situation was giving her more food for thought about what she'd have to do if she wanted to keep calling herself a musician.

But it'd be nice to come out of this trip with something to remember it and Noel by.

CHAPTER 4

THEY'D CROSSED the border into Manitoba and were coming up on Virden when Noel spotted a dark lump on the side of the highway. With Merrily concentrating on the road and the traffic in the dimming light, he pointed it out immediately. "Looks like somebody had a breakdown."

A dark pick-up was pulled as far to the shoulder as it could get. At first, he thought it had been abandoned and that the driver had already been taken into town, but then he saw something inside move. "They're still in there," he said in surprise.

"The engine wasn't running," Merrily said. Left unspoken was the fact it was well below freezing. Whoever it was wouldn't last long in the cold. She was already pressing the brakes.

"They'll be okay for another twenty minutes. We can send a tow-truck when we get to Virden. You don't need to stop."

"If the garage has one. If they aren't on another call. If

they haven't been stranded out there for an hour without gas already because people keep thinking the next guy is going to stop," she said. "Even with all of our stuff, there's room for a person in the backseat. If we need to make a second trip, I'll drop you at the hotel first and come back."

"You're not dropping me anywhere." He wasn't about to let her pick up a hitchhiker on her own.

It took her some time to find a place to make a U-turn, and then a longer make a second one and approach the truck again. This time, when Merrily pulled in directly behind the car, her headlights fully lit the back of the pick-up and filled the interior.

A figure turned and stared at them from driver's side of the bench seat. The door flew open, and the interior light spilled onto the road, illuminating a giant of a man who kept growing as he stepped out of the car.

"How did he even fit in there?" she wondered.

The man was massive, with bushy blonde hair sticking out from beneath a green cap with a gold logo. Hints of a scruffy blonde beard appeared around the edges of the scarf that was wrapped around his face. "Are you sure about this? What if he's a serial killer?" Noel asked.

"Look at him. The only thing serial killing he's ever done is on a box of Cap'n Crunch." In the spirit of the season, Noel admitted that the guy's unzipped jacket shook like a bowl full of jelly as the man hustled to Merrily's window.

"Hey, buddy, are you okay?" she asked.

"Cold, mostly. You're the first one to stop," the stranger said.

"Have you called anyone, or do you need a ride into town? We can drop you at a garage or take you to a hotel."

"I have family a couple blocks off Main Street. Is there any chance of getting a lift? It's just me and a bag full of presents. The rest can wait until I get my brother to drive me back."

"No problem," Merrily said.

Noel shivered when she closed the window. "I take it back. He's probably not a serial killer."

Their new passenger had to contort himself to fit in the back seat, even after Noel had pulled his seat forward as far as he could. "I appreciate this. Tommy Litzer is my name. Who do I have to thank for this roadside rescue?"

"I'm Merrily Sweet and this is my navigator, Noel Sprouse. At your service."

"You two are godsends."

"It's just a few kilometres." Merrily merged back into traffic.

Tommy shook his head. "Yeah, but I didn't want to walk it. I don't know what happened. That old Ford has always served me well. I just had her serviced. I can't believe poor Patrice up and died so close to home."

"You named your truck Patrice?"

"It's a good name."

Noel wasn't going to argue. He'd never named any of his vehicles, but if he had, Patrice wouldn't have made the list. "Well, sit back and get warm. We'll have you home in no time."

Tommy Litzer gave them easy directions to follow. His destination was, as he said, two blocks of the main road. "I can't thank you enough. Have a wonderful Christmas. Where are you headed?"

"The hotel up the highway tonight. Winnipeg tomorrow," Merrily said.

"Have a safe trip. And thanks again."

"You're welcome, Tommy. Have a merry Christmas with your family."

When they checked into the motel, Noel overheard the manager describing Merrily's room to her. She had a large double off an interior corridor, a view of the park behind the motel, and a coffee pot. He, however, had booked whatever they'd had left that morning, so he had a walk outside to a room that faced the highway and received apologies for having a broken coffee pot, although he did get a voucher for a free coffee the next morning from the diner across the parking lot. He didn't grumble much; finding a room this close to Christmas was a miracle in itself. If it was warm and clean, he could make do.

They dropped their baggage and met up at the diner for a quick bite before it closed. He took advantage of their free Wi-Fi to contact his family. *"Still on track to catch my flight tomorrow afternoon. Is Mom making shortbread?"*

The response he got burst his bubble from a good deed done. *"Are you sure you don't have something to tell us? How did you get Christmas off in your first year working for the company?"* What his father really meant was "Have you been fired already and are you afraid to tell us?"

Not wanting the suspicion to poison his mother's mind before he got home, he sent one more text. *"My boss had to cancel his holiday plans, so he took the Christmas shift this year and told me to go. You have my flight details. Will text if anything changes."*

Merrily slipped into the seat across from him. "You look ready to strangle somebody. What's up? Flight cancelled?"

"Bite your tongue. I don't need that kind of negative energy." He tried to make his voice teasing. "My dad was being my dad. He's absolutely convinced I'm going to lose this job by goofing around, just like I did the others, so he warned me to stay in line."

"Lose your job? Does he know that North Pole Unlimited sent you to an international conference? Nick said you were at the largest IT conference in Canada, and that it was a huge deal. I know that conference tied up traffic all over Vancouver and took over several hotels and the biggest convention centre in the city. Not to mention, you also created a cool app while holding down a full-time job. You've been working overtime lately."

Noel shook his head. There was no way he was telling his family about Christmas Every Day now. He wouldn't be able to sit through a meal of turkey and stuffing while listening to his family warn him about the danger of a new shiny idea trying to sneak past him on the inside. He needed to prove that he could focus before they'd accept that he could multitask on two different jobs.

"That sucks, Noel." She didn't offer more sympathy than that. She couldn't since she didn't know his family at all. But it was nice to have at least one person on his side.

"Speaking of the app, did you happen to notice what was hanging from Tommy Litzer's radio antenna?" he asked.

She grinned. "I did. A tiny little Christmas stocking. It was flapping like a flag. There was an almost identical blue truck in Vancouver when I picked you up at your hotel in Vancouver. At first, I thought it was the same truck, but the drivers looked completely different."

"You know, I was getting a little worried on your behalf about today's task, but luck came through at the last minute. Your success rate is three for three. I think it's a sign."

"I agree. I can't wait for tomorrow's assignment."

CHAPTER 5

December 22ⁿᵈ
Winnipeg, Manitoba

"Well, this is it. Good-bye. Again." The wind howled along the front of Winnipeg's international airport, blowing gusts of sharp ice crystals into any exposed skin. Merrily didn't need to get out of the car to see Noel off, but she wanted to. He'd made a difficult trip a lot easier. She had pulled out her notebook again the previous night in Virden. She hadn't come up with any breakthroughs, but she felt like she was getting closer to something she could turn into a song. It would probably have something about all the wishful thinking she'd been doing.

"I can't believe we made it," he said. "I'm glad that I sent my presents ahead. We would have been late if we'd had to drive down to December to pick them up first." He shivered when a gust blew into his unbuttoned coat.

"Get inside and out of the cold, Noel. Thanks for

being such a good navigator. And a good listener." He may not be ready to release Christmas Every Day, but he was actively working on it. It made her think that maybe it wouldn't matter if the songs she wrote were just for her until she got her confidence back.

"Thanks for saving my bacon. Twice. Merry Christmas to you and your family." Noel hesitated, then stepped forward and gave her a quick hug. "You're amazing. I enjoyed every kilometre with you. I hope you find some song-writing inspiration in your stocking for Christmas," he whispered in her ear.

"You're pretty special, too. I hope I can buy your app next year," she whispered back.

He'd made it to the door before she yelled at him. "Hey, Noel! What is today's Christmas Every Day task?"

"Give someone a compliment."

"Got it! I'll let you know how this one works out on the morning before the day before the night before Christmas. Bye, Noel."

The forty-five-minute drive from Winnipeg toward the American border was a cold trip. Wind blew across the highway, polishing drifts into ice. The grey clouds in the air threatened more snow. But Merrily was undeterred. She'd promised to visit the North Pole Unlimited complex on her cross-country tour and she intended to. She wanted to meet her new colleagues in person.

Signage on December's primary thoroughfare directed her to the main building where a friendly receptionist greeted her when she entered the building.

"Hi. I'm Merrily Sweet, and I'm here to see Nick Klassen."

She'd been shocked out of her socks when the vice-president of Human Resources contacted her personally to ask if she wanted to participate in the company's Christmas album. She'd thought it had been a joke; another guy trying to set himself up with a date with the popstar, especially when he called himself her number one fan.

Merrily had put Nick through so many hoops that she was surprised that he hadn't given up. Thankfully, he took her caution with good grace and once he'd proven who he said he was, they'd gotten on wonderfully. This was the first chance she'd have to meet him in person.

"I thought Nick was joking. It is you! I saw you in concert once. I'm Barb, by the way."

Merrily saw the way the woman's hand hovered above her camera. She knew that move. "Hi, Barb. It's nice to meet you. I hope you enjoyed the concert."

"It was for my twentieth birthday. I went home hoarse from screaming. Nick—Mr. Klassen—said that we shouldn't—"

"I love your holiday sweater. Can we take a picture together?" Merrily interrupted. Barb was wearing a knit pullover with a yoke of gold bells and holly leaves. It was Christmassy without being garish. While it was honestly nice, it was mostly an excuse. Nick had obviously warned his staff not to act like autograph hounds. Merrily appreciated it, but it wasn't necessary. It didn't happen much at all anymore.

"Are you sure you don't mind?"

"Absolutely." Merrily arranged them with the lobby's Christmas tree as their backdrop. She'd noticed an increase in the number of Likes she was receiving on her social media accounts, so she decided to post her own photo with a link to her Christmas album. ***Stopping in reception at North Pole Unlimited to discuss my latest songs and met Barb of the awesome pullover #HolidaySweater #NorthPoleUnlimited #NewSongsForAnOldfashionedChristmas #Roadtripping.***

As Barb returned to her desk to answer a phone, Merrily finished looking around the lobby. Somehow the lighting made the floor dance with green and red sparkles. An enormous Christmas tree filled an entire corner. A long row of white and red poinsettias lined a shelf that ran around the far side of the waiting room. Even the painting on the wall was of a reindeer in a winter scene.

"Mr. Klassen will be right out."

"Thanks, Barb."

The sound of scuffling feet drew her attention down the hall. A tall blonde Viking of a man and a short brown-haired woman were walking side by side. He would lengthen his stride and speed up, then she would skip ahead. By the time they reached the lobby, the pair were sprinting.

"Merrily! Can I call you Merrily? It's awesome to finally meet you in person. I'm Nick." His long steps brought him across the lobby three steps in front of the woman he was racing. He offered his hand, and then pumped hers enthusiastically. "Everybody is very excited that you're here for a visit. Don't tell anyone but your contributions to the album are my favourite. 'I'll Be Home For Christmas' is my favourite carol. While you're here, I'm hoping to talk you into doing at least two new ones for next year's album. Can you stay for lunch? We can give you a tour and finish in the cafeteria. It's world class. Literally. We've won awards."

"Nick! Let the poor girl catch her breath. Hi, I'm Jilly Lewis-Fredericks. We've spoken on the phone."

"It's nice to meet you in person, Jilly."

Nick stepped forward again. "We really appreciate that you stepped up to help Noel like you did. It was a big favour to ask. Did he make his flight on time today?" he asked.

"I dropped him off at the airport on my way here. He should be sitting outside his gate as we speak."

"Come with me. Let's talk about your next contract. After that, Ginger Malone in Marketing is dying to meet you. She's hoping you'll take a few photos for the company's social media accounts. Then Tim Hill in Entertainment is insisting that you stop by for eggnog and thanks. The whole department has voted you Elf of the Month in your honour since sales of 'New Songs for an Old-Fashioned Christmas' are double what our last Christmas album was. Apparently, there's been a new sales spike over the last couple days that he's attributing to your cross-country trip. Something about Mac the Moose?"

Jilly stepped forward. "But first, how was your trip? We ask, because we know you've been on the road for three straight days and that's stressful for anyone, isn't it, Nick? I can put out some coffee and cookies in Nick's office, although they'll be store-bought since *somebody* put a limit on our online orders."

"I'd love to take you up on the coffee after we get the work stuff out of the way, Jilly."

"I'll start a fresh pot and pull out the processed cookies." Jilly shot a disappointed look at her boss and stormed down the hall.

Nick fell into step beside Merrily. "Did you get them?" he asked quietly.

"Three dozen. In a bag in my trunk. Kris wrote 'Jilly' in big letters on the side, so you'll have to be careful to keep it out of sight," she whispered back. When Jilly looked back over her shoulder, Merrily returned to normal volume. "I'm hesitant to ask, but what is 'Elf of the Month'. Is it an award you only give out in December?"

"E. L. F. stands for 'Employee Leading the Field.' Those nominated have excelled on a project or goal in their department." He turned and led her into an office where several boxes of paper had exploded. Stacks of files were everywhere. Nick saw her horror and laughed. "Jilly needed two more filing cabinets, and she's moving files from the old one to the new ones. It's a process, or so she tells me. But ignore the mess and come on through to my office."

His office was stuffed with gift bags which covered his treadmill and the television stand along the wall. "Let's talk music and songs and what you'd be interested in doing for next year's North Pole Unlimited Christmas album." Nick gave her an assessing glance when she took a deep breath. "Do you already have an idea?"

She did. And it was all Noel's fault. She couldn't encourage him to bring Christmas Every Day to market when she wasn't willing to put any of her ideas on the line. "I am not promising you a brand-new Christmas song for next year, because I don't have one written. I don't even have an idea for one. But if I do come up with something, would you be interested in a Merrily Sweet original?" Her drive through the Rockies and across the prairies had sparked her brain a couple of times. If she could kindle that, she might get her imagination firing again.

"An exclusive song by Merrily Sweet? Of course, we'd be interested."

"Right now, it's an idea about an idea. Don't get too excited yet," she warned.

"Too late. I'll draft something up for original material this afternoon and file it for the second you're ready. And I'll let Contracts know that you're interested in working with us again next year. Was there anything else we should discuss, or would you like that tour now?"

"The tour."

She had no idea that the North Pole Unlimited complex was so huge. They started at the massive warehouse and loading docks, then moved to the computerized Logistics department that kept track of every order and shipment around the globe. Nick's offices were right next to the Payroll department, with the Animal Care department at the far end.

The Research and Development labs and Art Department were in a different wing which was connected via a glassed-in walkway, although a roughly shovelled path also ran outside alongside the tunnel.

Nick introduced her to Ginger, an energetic redhead in the Marketing Department who arranged a quick photo shoot with her holding copies of the Christmas CD, which Merrily promptly cross-posted to her own social media. *It's beginning to sound a lot like Christmas #NorthPoleUnlimited #NewSongsForAnOldfashionedChristmas.* After that was a whirlwind tour through their print shop before Nick's stomach growled and he announced it was time for lunch.

The cafeteria and several conference rooms were in their own building in beside the main one. As they walked through the lobby into the cafeteria, Merrily paused in front of a giant bulletin board that filled an entire wall. Amid the posters for the local food drive and December's Winter Extravaganza Decorating Contest was a sign calling for nomination for E.L.F. of the Year. The picture showed a large crystal star on a base and had a five-digit figure underneath it. "What is that all about?"

"It's an innovator's award," Nick said. "Anybody in any department or subsidiary can nominate themselves or someone else. The requirements are based on independent suggestions for improvements to the North Pole Unlimited brand."

"Is it a project that you are assigned to do on the job, or something you work on independently?"

"Either, but it usually ends up being the latter. The best innovations seem to be inspired by a person's day job but not part of their actual job description."

"I see." That was exactly what Noel needed. He'd have to do more research, but his app filled the requirements listed on the poster. It wasn't his job, but it was definitely inspired by where he worked. It was perfect.

"How was Mr. Sprouse as a passenger? I haven't had a chance to really get to know him yet," Nick said.

"He was great company. We had a fun trip together. I'm going to miss him riding shotgun. We'd never met before, but I knew of him from when he was still racing. Noel couldn't say enough good things about his job here. I think even he is surprised by how much he likes computer work after racing cars." She understood the excitement of trying something new. She liked that she and Noel had that passion in common.

"That may be so, but I'm still not going up against him in Mario Kart."

"That's probably best. I wouldn't either," she agreed.

The cafeteria meal was everything she'd been promised. The line cooks rivalled the best diner anywhere, and the buffet-style offerings were just as good. After her early morning and cold drive, Merrily had opted for the shepherd pie, then smothered it in gravy. The tasty, layered casserole of beef, vegetables, and mashed potatoes chased away the last of the chill that had plagued her in the Lemon Mobile.

"This has been great, but I have to go. I have another eight hours in the car today," Merrily said after her tray had been cleared away. "It was lovely to meet you all in person."

"Come on. I'll walk you to your car."

Exhaust belched from the tailpipe when Merrily started her van from the lobby. "Thanks for everything, Nick. I really enjoyed working on 'New Songs for an Old-Fashioned Christmas,' and I can't wait to see what we do next year."

Nick walked to the car with her. "I'm glad you said yes. Look, I know I threatened the staff not to swamp you with photo requests, but is there any chance..."

"Of course. I'm not going to say no to a selfie with the boss," she joked. "Let's do it inside in front of the tree." With the photo taken, her ski jacket zipped, and the bag from Calgary safely transferred to Nick's vehicle, Merrily crossed her fingers that the interior of her van was warm enough to get her comfortably on the road.

"Wait!" Jilly raced into around the reception desk. "I'm so glad I caught you. How would you feel about a passenger for the second half of your trip?"

Merrily didn't try to stop the frown. Doing one favour was fine, but everyone involved was lucky that it had gone as well as it had. Twenty-four hours in a car with a bad travelling companion could feel like a lifetime. She didn't want to test her luck a second time. "I'm sorry, Jilly, but I already have plans for the rest of my drive." Her week-long self-reflection time had already been cut in half. She had some serious life choices to make, and she deserved that time to herself.

"It's Noel, if that makes a difference."

"Noel? I swear I dropped him off in lots of time for his flight. It was listed as 'on time' when he arrived."

Jilly pulled out her phone and showed her and Nick the screen. It was an off-centred picture of Noel holding a paper napkin to his bleeding nose and one puffy eye that was already shifting from red to purple.

"What on earth happened to him? Did the plane crash?"

"He's refusing to give details other than the fact there was a scuffle at the gate, the pilot and one flight attendant were injured, and the flight has been cancelled since there is no back-up crew available."

"There are no other big airports east between here and Ottawa for him to catch another flight, and I'm not backtracking to Regina for him. I'm sorry but no. I'll never make it home in time for Christmas." She liked Noel, she really did. But she wasn't going to give up her Christmas so a guy she'd met three days ago could have his. She'd already gone above and beyond.

"I don't know what he's suggesting. If he does have a back-up flight booked, we didn't do it. It's December 22nd. As good as I am, even I can't conjure commercial flight seats out thin air. He asked if you were still around, and if you'd call him before you left."

"I'll text him," she promised. From the privacy of her van where she'd be less worried about coming off like a jerk if she had to leave him stranded in Winnipeg. At least he could make it back to his home in December and not be stuck in a hotel room for the holidays.

"Noel, what's up?"

"A curling brawl broke out at the gate while we were loading the plane. It took down the captain and one of the flight attendants."

Merrily blinked at her phone. *"Sorry. Did you say a curling brawl? I need details."*

"Later? Just know police were called, pilot left in an ambulance, and flight was cancelled. How would you feel about a navigator all the way through to Ottawa?"

"Don't you mean Montreal?" she typed.

"I'm already begging you to drive me across the entire country. My family can get in the car for two hours to pick me up from Ottawa if they want me home that badly."

Going back to Winnipeg and picking him up was going to add another hour to her already long, eight-hour afternoon and evening drive. She didn't know if she could do it.

Although, she would have a professional driver in the car with her to spell her if she needed it. She knew Noel would agree if she asked. *"Are you willing to do some of the driving? The northern route over Lake Superior is a miserable, slow, careful drive at the best of times. This is not the best of times."*

"I'd treat your Lemon Mobile like it was my own car."

"I've seen what's left of your race cars when you're done with them, Noel."

"LOL. I'll treat it like it was my mother's car."

Her thinking time would be out the window. On the other hand, her conversations with Noel promised to be much more inspirational than her unproductive navel-gazing. That wasn't a con on any list. *"Do you realize it's two more days of driving?"*

"I'm game if you're willing."

"Have donut holes and hot chocolate waiting when I give you the 'I'll be there in 10 minutes' warning."

It appeared she was going to have company for the next twenty-five hundred kilometres.

INTERLUDE

North Pole Unlimited
    December, Manitoba

"Nick Klassen, you are the best boss ever. I've told you that, right?" Jilly Lewis-Fredericks said, wiping cookie crumbs from her lips before she grabbed another chocolate meringue from the Totally Iced box on her desk.

"I'm glad to hear my hard work and planning has kept me in the number one spot. Especially since I know that at least three other people ordered you the same cookies," Nick retorted. Providing Jilly with her favourite seasonal treats from Calgary was a simple but effective way to keep on the good side of the woman who controlled payroll, and he wasn't the only person to take advantage of her weakness for them.

"I pride myself on being easy to buy for." She stared at the last cookie in the box and reluctantly offered it to him.

"I'm good, thanks." Nick snickered at her look of

relief. He'd taken one when she'd offered their first year working together; he hadn't repeated the mistake.

"Did you finally get Eve's gift wrapped?" she asked.

He'd borrowed another roll of tape from her desk. It had been a really big box. "Eventually. Plus, I got my close, personal friend Merrily Sweet to autograph her debut album's CD case, so I have one gift she won't be able to guess."

"Did she personalize it to you, or to Eve?"

"It was my CD. She wished Eve a merry Christmas." That's how he knew he was crazy in love about his wife. He was gifting her one of his most prized possessions. The loss was balanced by the fact that he'd met Merrily in person and would be talking to her on a regular basis. They'd had lunch together and didn't discuss business at all, so he could say that they'd hung out as friends. "Relatedly, I think I know why you were laughing. I accidentally pulled a partial Jilly on Merrily, didn't I?"

His assistant's eyebrows hit her hairline. "Pulled a partial Jilly?"

"When I asked Merrily to drive Noel Sprouse to Calgary. I didn't know they'd hit it off so well. She talked about him a lot over lunch. I have the feeling my interference and introduction might have accidentally started something between them. You, on the other hand, plot and interfere on purpose."

"And I do an excellent job at it. All my matches are still together. Look at you and Eve." Jilly snatched the cookie box off her desk. "I'm not going to offer you any more cookies until we find out if your matchmaking attempt bears fruit. I've been an exemplary example for six years, demonstrating all kinds of techniques to keep two people together until their common sense kicks in and they realize who they have. If you haven't picked up any tips by now, there's no hope for you. You have till Christmas. Then I'll have to take over."

He couldn't subject his good friend Merrily to a full Jilly matchmaking onslaught. "I trapped them in a vehicle together for two entire days. And I still have two days till Christmas. I can still pull this off." Nick was ninety percent sure that Merrily would be happy with the results, and Noel seemed like a good guy from what he remembered.

He could definitely pull this off.

CHAPTER 6

"You NEVER DID GIVE me the details of what exactly happens during a curling brawl."

Noel moved the donut box into position when Merrily reached blindly for a donut hole, then offered her a napkin. "Do I have to?" he whined. His mouth, cheek and eye still ached, even after taking a couple of painkillers.

"Yes. I must know. Hockey players brawl. Soccer fans brawl. Curlers don't do anything more than yell."

"Oh, they brawl." He poked gently at his eye. "We had two teams booked on our flight. Apparently, team one had been forced to check their brooms while the other team had collapsible ones and were going to put them in the overhead bins. When team one found out about team two, they started yelling about how it was a conspiracy to lose their brooms in transit and how team two had to check their brooms to keep it even."

"I told you there would be yelling."

"Then," he continued, "team one decided that if team

two wouldn't hand over their brooms voluntarily to be checked, they'd do it for them."

"And that's when the fight broke out?" They both chuckled at the old joke.

"It would have been bad enough getting hit in the face with an old-fashioned straw broom, but these new ones are freaking solid. The pilot was waiting to board and tried to separate the skips, and team one's lead clocked him right in the side of the head. The poor pilot bounced off the boarding desk before he hit the floor."

"What happened to you?" Merrily asked.

He held his hands in front of him, like he was holding onto a stick. "Two people were fighting over a broom. The skinny handle end caught one of the flight attendants right in the ribs. I tried to catch her on her way down and caught the broom on the side of my head."

"Ouch. Then what happened."

"Security arrived at the same time as the on-duty police in the airport. Now eight people will be asking Santa for bail money this Christmas and everybody on the flight had to make alternate travel arrangements."

"It would be funny if nobody had been hurt. I wonder if it'll make the national news tonight."

The first three hours of the drive flew by as he contacted his family to tell them that he'd yet again had to change his itinerary. He'd gone over his and Merrily's new timetable as they made their way out of the city. He and Merrily had another twenty-five hundred kilometres to cover. They'd knock off eight hundred before they stopped that night in Thunder Bay on the north-west shore of Lake Superior. Tomorrow they'd circle the entire north shore of the largest lake in North America by driving on a skinny two-lane highway through relentless, rocky wilderness with storms that could blow off the lake at any time. The trip was challenging in the summer. He'd never tried it in the winter. If Merrily was going to trust him with her vehicle, he was going to be the safest driver on the highway.

Merrily pulled off the highway when the signs for Kenora, Ontario became more frequent. "Rest break?" he asked.

"In a few minutes. I have to visit with an old friend first."

It was just after four, but it was almost full dark since the sun set early in the longest days of December. She pulled to a stop in the roadside park, with the headlights angled toward Lake of the Woods...and a towering forty-foot fish statue. "Really?"

"Noel Sprouse, meet my BFF in Kenora. It's too cold to do a full photo shoot, but can you get a few of me and my buddy?"

"Why not. Every man wants to know he comes second to a big fish," he joked.

The photos he took showed clouds of condensation as Merrily exhaled in the evening air. It hadn't warmed up at all since they'd left Winnipeg. He'd started following her social media, so he knew when she posted her latest stop. He gave a heart to "*I went ice fishing and caught a fish this big! #HuskieTheMusky #Kenora #LakeOfTheWoods #Roadtripping.*"

The bracing photo stop, and a quick break for fuelling up her Lemon Mobile and themselves left them ready to go a little after five o'clock. Clouds in the pitch-dark sky blotted out any hope of star or moon light.

"How would you feel about doing this next stretch?"

Merrily asked. "Thunder Bay is about five hours from here. It's going to be a long drive."

"It's not a problem." Contrary to his reputation, Noel didn't mess around with his cars off the track. The accident that had ended his career had been a combination of bad weather and a novice bus driver.

As the road stretched into the darkness and Merrily's instrumental Christmas playlist played in the background, their surface get-to-know-you conversations began to drift to deeper topics. "Why are you asking me about Christmas Every Day again? It's not even a real thing," Noel said again.

"Because it's a fantastic idea and I think it would be really popular. Did you know you could put submit it for North Pole Unlimited's Elf of the Year Innovator's award? You should check it out."

She was amazing. He'd never imagined so much support from someone he just met. Merrily felt like his own private cheering section. One he didn't deserve. "It's a goofy little thing I put together for my aunts. I can't show it to my bosses."

"Why not? You said it was finished. The ideas are cute. When you first described it, I thought they'd be pretty complex and time consuming, but they're easy. From what you've described, some of them even verge on passive, like the 'tell a holiday joke' ones. Those are a great option, so people don't get overwhelmed with activities."

"I repeat, they're goofy."

"That's the point, isn't it? You wanted your aunts to have fun. How advanced have you made the app? Is there a way you can mark a day's task as completed? Can you go back and do a previous activity if you miss a day and still have it count?" she asked. She knew she'd forget, but she'd probably do it regularly in December. Thirty-one cute Christmas ideas wouldn't be too onerous.

"Yes to both. Apps have better user experiences and more subscribers if they're gamified. Every time you do fifteen tasks, it adds an ornament to your digital Christmas tree." He'd been proud of himself when he'd come up with that concept. Merrily kept using words like "cute" and "fun". That's all it was it was. His app wasn't going to change the world or revolutionize North Pole Unlimited's business structure. All it would do was add some Christmas cheer to its users' lives.

He must have said that last line out loud. "Exactly!" Merrily agreed. "These days, people need all the Christmas cheer they can get, whenever they can get it."

"It's not that easy to put your baby out there. If it was, you'd be sharing the music you've been writing in the evening. I'd love to hear it. I promise to be supportive," Noel countered. It had been a leap of trust for him to tell her about Christmas Every Day. The least she could do was reciprocate.

She went silent for ten kilometres. "Okay," she agreed. "Tomorrow."

CHAPTER 7

DECEMBER 23RD
Thunder Bay, Ontario

Merrily gripped the steering wheel extra hard, and it was not because a semi had just passed them on the winding highway at the top of Lake Superior. Beside her in the passenger seat, Noel had just listened to her thirty second music clip for the fourth time. "It's terrible, right? I warned you it was bad. That's why I shared it first, so the next one would sound better."

Noel nodded his head slowly. "Yes, you did say that. And you're right. It does sound like Grandma June's chicken jingle."

"See!" Perhaps she'd been hungry while she'd been working on it, because with a few minor changes, she could be singing about falling in love with deep fried drumsticks.

"But that doesn't mean it's bad," Noel continued. "I think you're selling yourself short."

Noel was undeniably cute, and a quick glance showed his brown eyes to be sincere, but he obviously knew nothing about music. "It's not salvageable. Believe me, I tried."

"Not as a song," he agreed. "This idea is a little out there, but is there a reason you can't sell it to Grandma June as a radio ad?"

"A radio jingle?" Her voice squeaked at the thought. That was a blow to her artistic soul. "That is very commercial. Literally, even."

"Money talks. Everything else walks because they don't have the funds for bus fare," Noel said. "Believe me, I know. I went from stock car driver to midnight shelf stocker when I went back to school. But it paid the bills. Nobody has to know it came from you if you don't want them to."

Even her ego had to admit it made sense. It would be great fodder in her memoirs once she was topping the music charts again, and until then, it might pay the rent. "I'll think about it."

"If that's the first, what's the second?" Noel asked.

Merrily's heart dropped into her stomach. She knew the first sample was bad. But this one was what she'd come up with after her drive through the prairies. There'd been the nugget of an idea there, and she'd worked on it all night after her foolish promise to Noel. She was supposed to be encouraging him; she didn't know how she'd ended up being encouraged back.

"It's one verse and a chorus. Maybe. I don't know what I think of it, but I promised to share, so just play it." If he hated it, she'd pull over and let him drive as she crawled into the backseat and hid with her coat over her head in embarrassment. She'd hadn't been so worried about a song in years.

Noel played it. Then played it again. "There's a rest stop up ahead. Can you pull over?" he requested. Then he played it a third time.

She was going to be sick. He was going to tell her it sucked, and he didn't want her to burst into tears while she was driving. Her breath hitched as she eased to the shoulder and into the small parking pad. "You hated it. I knew you'd hate it." She shouldn't even be doing jingles. She needed to go home and get a job in a library where she'd never have to sing again.

"Merrily, will you stop? It's good!"

"It's terrible."

"It's good. It's upbeat, it's got a good vibe. I think you've made a solid start."

"It's not done," she protested. The lyrics were still a bit off and the bridge to the chorus was jagged. It was several steps below good.

"I know that. Merrily, I basically challenged you to write a song overnight. I'm not expecting a chart-topper after a full day of driving. But you did it. You started a song—what promises to be a good song," he elaborated. "Aren't you at all pleased with yourself? I thought you said you hadn't written in a year. Now you're writing again. That's huge. You should be proud, not in tears."

"It's not good."

"It's a start. You started."

She wanted to believe. "What if I can't make it good?" Merrily had suffocated her musical side for the last year, out of fear and pride. Letting life flow back to it was triggering painful pins and needles in her brain. She was afraid to put her heart back into her music in case nobody wanted it again.

"Then you play with different notes and write another song. Christmas Every Day wasn't the first app I tried to build, you know. I have a dozen failed attempts at various racing apps that I thought were good ideas but eventually I found something I could make work. You will make this work. This is day three since you started writing again. Give yourself some grace, Merrily."

She sniffed. Loudly. "Thank you."

"Now switch seats with me. I don't think that you should be driving for a while."

She didn't either. She was still shaking from the stress of sharing her music. The fresh air took her breath away as she walked around the vehicle, and the cold breeze set her cheeks tingling. Somewhere deep inside, Merrily acknowledged that fear and excitement felt a lot alike.

It was too bad she only had Noel around for another day. He was sweet. Supportive.

And he didn't cut her any slack when she started running herself down. She needed that.

The next thing she knew the van was rolling to a stop. They were on the side of the highway, the sound of cars and trucks rolling by audible now that they'd stopped moving. Merrily brought her seat fully upright to look around. "Where are we?"

"I figured you absolutely had to say hello to an old friend here. Was I right?"

She blinked and looked around. There, in front of the van, was a massive steel statue of a Canada goose. "Are we in Wawa already?"

"Unless there's a second town along the Trans-Canada Highway home to a giant goose, yes."

"I didn't realize I'd slept that long." She shouldn't be so surprised. She'd stayed up past midnight trying to mold a whisp of an idea into a song, and then they'd had a cold and early start on the next leg of their journey when she'd been a complete emotional mess about Noel. She'd been exhausted by the time she got in the van. But apparently not only her song efforts had merit, but she'd also trained Noel to take advantage of interesting rest stops. "But I'm grateful I have another photo opp."

"Does this fowl beast have a name?"

"I've heard that it's Wally, but everybody I know just calls it the Wawa Goose. Do you want me to take a picture of you? You can send it to your parents to let them know that you're getting closer to your final destination." Noel was taking extreme measures to get home for Christmas. The least his family could do was acknowledge he was trying to make it happen. None of his delays were his fault. His kindness and support only ensured that she was determined he was going to make it home on time.

They were fortunate that their rest stop was under a patch of blue sky. They'd finally outdriven the endless snowstorm. It was the first time Merrily had seen anything but clouds in days. "Do you think this good weather will last all the way to Ottawa?" she asked hopefully.

Noel finished posing and they hustled back to the van. "Sadly not. There's another storm blowing in from the east coast. All of New York state is getting clobbered at the moment. It's coming."

"Then let's go." They had miles to go before they could sleep.

After she adjusted the seat so she could reach the pedals, she turned up the volume on the speakers that

Noel had reduced to barely audible. "Let's get find travel-ling music." When Tom Cochrane's "Life is a Highway" began playing, she knew the rest of their trip was going to be alright.

CHAPTER 8

THE BREAK in the weather didn't last long. Merrily spent the last hundred kilometres hunched over the steering wheel, squinting into the distance while the driving snow made it feel like they were entering hyperdrive in a science fiction movie. Noel did his part by not distracting her. When they finally pulled into the motel in Sudbury, Noel couldn't help but breathe a sigh of relief that they were off the highway.

"I'm going to spend an hour in a hot shower to get the kinks out of my neck," Merrily muttered. "That was a miserable drive." Then she smiled at him, and the blustery weather didn't matter. "But the company was fantastic."

That made him feel better. When Noel had made the deal with Merrily to share her music, he had no idea he was going to trigger a nervous breakdown. He just wanted to hear what she was working on now. The idea of making a living by creating music was so completely foreign and exciting to him that he wanted to hear all about it. Her brain had to be a wonderous place to be.

The fact that she told him that she felt the same way about his app was unbelievable. But when something was new and interesting, he understood wanting to know everything about it.

It wasn't about her being famous. They'd both had time in the spotlight. He loved how much she loved her music. She gave it one hundred percent of her energy—unless she was singing along to the radio and that was only about fifty percent. He'd never had a road trip pass so quickly, except this last stretch when he was worried for her.

After they'd checked in and were watching the wind batter the windows, Noel took a good look around the lobby. "Merrily, have you stayed here before?" he asked quietly.

"No, but it had decent ratings online. Why?"

He nodded his head toward the corner of the room, where a dust bunny the size of a boot resided behind a plastic chair. Three dead plants decorated the windowsill, and an orange plastic pylon sat in the middle of a puddle beside the check-in desk.

She shrugged. "Hopefully the rooms are good. It's not like we have much choice. Did you see how full the parking lots were at the other two hotels we passed?"

"Fingers crossed," he said, but he didn't have much hope. He didn't need fancy, but Noel wanted to be clean and warm and fed.

He got two out of three. When he opened his door, he spotted a thin layer of ice coating the window overlooking the highway. Condensation freezing onto window glass wasn't completely unexpected, but it did say something about the temperatures outside and in the room. He dropped his suitcase on the bed, turned up the thermostat, and trudged down the concrete sidewalk to meet Merrily for the trek to the restaurant.

"Hey, look!" Merrily pointed to a familiar-looking blue truck in the diner's parking lot. The stocking on the antenna was barely more than lump of snow. "What on earth is Tommy Litzer doing here? He said his family was in Virden."

"Maybe he was just staying with them for the night. It's weird that we ran into him again, though. We should say hi and make sure Patrice hasn't given him any more problems." Noel appreciated the lines of a classic truck; it wasn't exactly his style, but he was a little jealous of the blue beauty.

They entered the loud, bustling restaurant and saw the back of a large man in a green and gold toque and big scarf. "Hi, Tommy," he said. When the man didn't respond, Noel tried again. "Tommy Litzer?"

A man turned around and smiled. "Sorry, wrong person." It wasn't the same man they'd helped two nights before. Instead of a grizzled older man, this guy was young, fit, and clean-shaven.

"Our mistake," Merrily said. "We spotted a classic blue Ford outside and thought it belonged to a friend of ours, although we were wondering what he was doing so far from home".

"The truck is mine, so you were right on that front. I rebuilt it myself."

"It's amazing!"

Noel didn't realize that Merrily was so friendly. Yes, she'd first hit immediately hit it off with the baker in Calgary, and when she'd struck up a conversation with Tommy, and—yeah, he really should have put the pieces together sooner. Which was why he wasn't surprised when the hostess came to their group and asked if they wanted one table or two, and Merrily nudged his arm. "I'm Noel, and this is Merrily. Do you want to eat with us?" Noel asked. "If you don't have plans."

"That sounds a lot better than eating alone. Thank you."

Noel couldn't face another platter of fries and a burger, and the thought of chicken fingers elicited the same reaction from his stomach. When the waitress walked past with a tray full of chicken pot pies, he knew he'd found his answer. The smell was so enticing, all three of them ended up ordering it.

"I'm Martin, by the way. I've got to ask, have we met before?" their lunch guest asked.

And that was when Merrily, formerly as sweet as her name, threw him under the bus. "Since you're a truck guy, you might recognize Noel. Noel Sprouse. He retired as a top-rated stock car driver before he moved into I.T."

Martin's eyes went wide. "Yes, you were. Out of Montreal. The station covered some of your races when I was working there."

"Station?" Merrily asked.

"Radio station. I was doing P.R. in Montreal about six years ago. We covered a lot of local events. You were always big news."

Noel knew exactly what Martin meant. "Are you still in radio?" he asked, the glimmer of an idea forming.

"I host a late-night call-in show in Sudbury now."

"If you're in radio, you probably recognize Merrily too. She's Merrily Sweet, one of Canada's favourite pop stars."

Martin blinked. "You are. You really are," he realized,

laughing. "What are you two doing together in Sudbury of all places?"

They regaled him with their connection through North Pole Unlimited, their cross-country journey, and about how they still had one more travel day left. Martin thought the entire situation was hilarious, especially Noel's string of terrible travel luck. "You know, this would be an epic story for my listeners."

"Feel free," Merrily offered magnanimously.

"That's because you come out smelling like a rose and I come out of it stinking like runway moose and curling brooms," Noel grumbled, grinning.

The pot pie was excellent and the company hilarious as Martin recounted stories of some of the calls he'd received on his show, Noel reminisced about his favourite IT help requests, and Merrily discussed the group debates over which Christmas songs to sing—one of which resulted in a hair-pulling episode between two other contributors on the album.

Martin insisted on picking up the bill as thanks for not making him eat alone. They said their good-byes and went their separate ways. That's when things started to go downhill.

The storm had picked up, driving the pellet-like snow horizontally so hard they made noise when they struck the nylon coating of Merrily's jacket. He waited with her while she verified the Lemon Mobile's block heater was plugged in so the engine wouldn't be frozen solid in the morning, and they doubled over to fight the wind on the way back to their rooms. Noel dropped her off, then continue down the row to his door.

When he got inside, he shivered in relief to be out of the wind.

But it wasn't much warmer inside than outside. The ice on the windows had been joined by an inch of frost at the base of the motel room's exterior door. Before dinner, he'd cranked the thermostat over the regularly set eighteen to twenty-two Celsius, the thick red bar hovering over the seventy-two on the lower Fahrenheit scale. But the room itself was reading a chilly fifteen Celsius. Noel squinted to see a faded "60 F" beneath it. "This is ridiculous," he muttered to himself. Then the wind gusted again, and the frosted pane in the window rattled.

He picked up the phone to call the front desk. "Hi, it's Noel Sprouse in room twelve. I think my heater is broken. My room isn't warming up and hardly any heat is coming from the radiator." The excuse was terrible. "I'm sorry to hear your second boiler is broken, but there must be a way to heat the motel. Do you have space heaters?" It wasn't an ideal situation, but it was better than the alternative.

There was no alternative. He even tried calling other hotels in Sudbury. At two days before Christmas, there was no room at the inn, or the hotel, or the motel. Every place he tried was booked. He even made phone calls rather than trying to book online in case the managers were holding something in reserve, but between Christmas travellers and curling teams in town for an inter-provincial tournament, nothing was available. Noel shivered; he'd be better off sleeping in Merrily's van. The thin comforter and the single blanket on the closet shelf weren't going to be warm enough.

He was trying to come up with a third option when there was a knock at his door. When he opened it, Merrily pushed her way into his room. "Oh, you have heat, this is wonderful!"

"This isn't heat. It's cold in here."

She stalked to his thermostat and bounced on her toes as she read it. "Sixteen degrees. That's four more than I have. I can't stay in my room."

"My room isn't much better, and there's nothing else in town. I checked."

"What are we going to do?"

He thought for a minute. "Option one is that we fuel up and start driving again. It's not ideal, but we'll be home twelve hours early. Option two is a little awkward." That was a lie. It was a lot awkward. "If you bring the blankets and comforter from your room into my room, we might have enough covers to stay warm if we're fully dressed under them in the same bed. I promise to be a complete gentleman."

"You'd have to be, or you'd be freezing parts off after I booted you out of the bed for trying something," she countered. "But freezing all night is not a good option either."

"People might talk."

"If people say that we should turn into blocks of ice to avoid the appearance of sin rather than safely stay warm while actually not sinning, they need to go back to church. I'm game if you are. I'm freezing."

"Sure. Go grab your blanket and comforter and I'll see if we can coax any more heat out of the radiator."

Changing clothes in a frosty bathroom wasn't much fun, but the clean T-shirt and socks made him feel fresher. Merrily returned minutes later, hauling her suitcase and a bundle of linens under her arm. Like him, she quickly came out of the bathroom with a t-shirt collar peeking out from under her hoodie and bright white socks going under her jeans legs. "If I had long johns, I would have put them on too. Even the hot water is only lukewarm. Only two stars, one for location and one for cleanliness. Do not recommend in the dead of winter." Her teeth chattered.

"Come on." He gestured at the bed that was a giant pile of pillows and blankets. "There's a Christmas movie marathon on the retro station. Eighties hair and shoulder pads."

"Wow, how can I turn down that?" Merrily joked.

With the pillows up against the headboard, it was almost like watching television together on a sofa that had footrests. He had the hood of his hoodie up, and Merrily had tied a scarf around her head. She'd dozed for a while but woke up again when church bells started pealing on the screen. Noel nodded off for a few minutes and missed the reunion of a pint-size hero and the family who'd accidentally left him behind on their family's Christmas vacation.

The credits were rolling when Merrily flipped to her side and stared at him. "I think I can see my breath in the room." Sure enough, when he checked the thermostat, it had dropped another two degrees.

"Even with the extra blankets, I don't think we'll make it till morning without getting sick," Noel admitted. He'd stretched out on the bed and had a nap, but there was no way he'd get a full night's sleep.

"What do you think of getting back on the road. Now?"

The clock on the bedside table said it was a little after one in the morning. It would take about five hours to get to Ottawa. That would give his parents lots of time to drive down from Montreal to pick him up and get back home in time for the Christmas eve carol service. Her suggestion would work out great... for him. "Are you sure? You didn't get much rest. Will you be okay to drive?"

"I think so. I'm fine right now. You might have to spell me for a nap, but I think we'd be better off driving than pretending to sleep here."

"Of course, I will if you need me to." Noel stared into her blue eyes, which were wide awake and burning with energy. "I'm going to have a very fast shower and get dressed. We can head out in fifteen minutes. Work for you?"

"Definitely. We'll find a twenty-four-hour restaurant, refuel and warm-up, say hello to Nicky on the way out of town, and be on the road before three. We—well, I—will be home by noon on Christmas eve. I love this plan!"

As Noel helped her gather her blankets to take back to her room, he asked the question that he knew had an obvious answer but was one he couldn't come up with. "Who's Nicky?"

CHAPTER 9

They'd lingered at the truck stop diner longer than Merrily had intended, but it was decadently warm in the restaurant and there was so much holiday anticipation in the air that she didn't want to leave at all. It was surprisingly packed for two in the morning. Little bits of conversation drifted to their booth from around the room. It seemed like everybody was in transit, and quite a few were heading east to Ottawa and beyond.

Merry pulled out her phone after they ordered and was immediately distracted by her exploding social media notifications. Apparently, Martin had taken them up on her offer and told their story to his listeners. She didn't think Martin expected his radio clips to go viral, but something had been picked up somewhere. All of a sudden, all her road trip posts were generating likes and shares. And comments! People seemed to love the idea of her and Noel crossing the country before Christmas.

"What is your social media doing?" she asked.

"Blowing up like yours. I haven't been on it much since I left racing. I seem to have picked up a lot of followers—an entire array of geeks who sympathize with my help desk question stories."

"I'd bet they'd also be supportive of a guy who was programming a new app," Merrily said. She returned his stare without flinching. She was running out of time to encourage him about Christmas Every Day. "But let's put away our phones. We should eat and get going."

The weather reports for those headed east were not promising. The cold front that was currently battering southern Ontario was moving slowly, leaving them with more wind, snow, and cold to battle through.

Merrily was undeterred. Her pancakes were steaming hot and fluffy, and her coffee was scalding, but what really warmed her heart was when Noel insisted on picking up the check, telling her that buying her a meal after their double feature was the least that he could do for a Christmas Eve non-date since they'd made it to the twenty-fourth.

Then they were finally on their way. Their travel mugs were filled to the brim: hers with hot chocolate for the sugar rush, Noel's with straight black coffee. The gas tank was full, and the heater had warmed the Lemon Mobile to a tolerable temperature. They just had one more stop to make before they started the final leg.

"We're in Sudbury. How can you not know who Nicky is?" she teased.

"I don't know anybody in Sudbury," Noel protested.

"What is Sudbury known for? What kind of friend

could I possibly have that wouldn't mind seeing me at three in the morning?"

"A very statuesque one?" he guessed.

"Ding, ding, ding. Please have your picture taking finger warmed up because we'll have to do this quickly before my nose falls off from the cold." She didn't do any funny poses in front of the Big Nickel, a thirty-foot coin that was a nod to Sudbury's mining industry. Standing in the light of the headlights, she gestured over her shoulder and Noel did the rest. He surprised her by taking a selfie of the two of them with the giant coin in the background. It wasn't the most attractive photo she'd ever had taken, with their hair sticking out from hoods and hats, clouds of vapour beside their faces, and shadows everywhere. But after all their time together, Merrily wouldn't swap it for a professional photo shoot for the world.

It was the final roadside attraction that was on her route to Ottawa without making a detour, and the weather and timing meant that she couldn't stray from the TransCanada. *Last stop before Christmas. I'll bet you a nickel you can't guess where we are #Sudbury #UncommonCents #HiMartin #Roadtripping.*

"There are less than six hours left on your road trip. What do you want to do? Besides giving me my Christmas Eve task of the day," she asked once they were back on the main highway heading east.

"Christmas Every Day says you must sing a carol on the night before Christmas," Noel read off his phone.

A mischievous grin spread across her face. "Are you easily embarrassed?"

"Considering how many times I crashed my own car, not really."

"Excellent."

"Why?" Noel asked, caution filling the van.

"No reason," she lied cheerfully. It was Christmas Eve, she was almost home, and she wanted to give Noel a Christmas present to remember her by. It would be risky, and it would be challenging to figure out the timing, but she might be able to pull it off.

They rolled east, the weather fighting them every kilometre. Wind buffeted the car, and the darkness loomed heavily even as it dumped endless snow on them. With the heaters on full, the inside of the Lemon Mobile was toasty warm, but they were not being fuel efficient. Without knowing when country gas stations would close on Christmas Eve, Merrily didn't want to risk running low.

She pulled into a well-lit gas station half an hour past North Bay that was serviced with a twenty-four-hour mini mart but no restaurant. A large, leaning passenger van was parked beyond the pumps, and she could see close to a dozen teenagers huddled in the store.

"It's my turn to fill the tank if you want to stretch," Noel offered.

"Do you want a cola?" After four days together in cramped quarters, she recognized the signs. His coffee had worn off a while back, and they still had hours to go. It was nice, although shocking, that she knew him so well already. Their entire trip could have been a disaster, but they'd gone the other way; they'd clicked in a way she'd never experienced before. If they weren't expected by family, she would have seriously considered getting lost to spend more time with him. Unfortunately, there were some lines she couldn't cross.

As she took her place at the end of the line of snack

seekers waiting to pay, she noticed that all the teens had the same sweaters on under their jackets. "You are all in a school choir?" she asked the young man standing in front of her.

"Yeah."

"What are you doing in the middle of nowhere in the middle of the night?"

"We were doing a show at a retirement home up the road in North Bay last night. The van gave us some problems when we started but we eventually got on the road. We got this far when the driver pulled over to check out a problem. It turns out we've got a flat and now we're stuck until we can get the tire changed. I heard Mr. Tanner talking to the tow truck guy. It's going to take forever for them to get out here, and we're stuck until then."

"That's a long night. I'll bet your audience appreciated you though."

"They were okay. So long as we get home this morning, it'll be Merry Christmas to us." They shuffled forward, and the black-haired boy squinted. "Do I know you?"

"I'm pretty sure we haven't met before."

"No, I know you."

"I'm Merrily Sweet."

"Holy cr—" He blinked. "I mean, wow, this is cool. And unexpected. Merry Sweet! We did one of your songs at regionals last year."

"I'm flattered. How'd you place?"

"Second in the province." It was a straight-up brag, no humbleness involved. Merrily approved. "I'm Tyler. Tyler Tran."

"Nice to meet you, Tyler."

"Is there any way you would take a picture with me and my choir? And Mr. Tanner, our choir director."

This was the timing Merrily was waiting for. "Maybe we can do each other a favour. I know it's been a long day for you, but do you think you have one more song in you?"

She returned to the Lemon Mobile to drop off their snacks, but Noel was nowhere to be found. She followed voices and found him crouched beside the passenger van, in deep discussion with another man.

"If you've got a spare, I can help you change it. It'll be faster than waiting."

"Do you know what you're doing? I don't mean to be rude, but I'm driving my students. I can't take any chances."

"I know," Noel assured him.

"He used to race cars," Merrily asked. "He knows his ways around vehicles."

"Do you have a jack?" Noel asked her quieter. "I can help, but it'll make us later."

She understood. "We can't say no. It's in the back. I'll have to move some stuff."

Noel turned to the other man. "Yes?"

"Yes," he said.

"I'll be right back." Merrily jogged to the Lemon Mobile. After some sweaty lifting and rearranging, she pulled out the jack out of its compartment and handed it over to Noel and the man he introduced as Mr. Tanner.

"We'll be a few minutes."

"Don't worry. I can keep myself occupied. I'll check on you in a bit." The delay gave her enough time to plan the day's Christmas task.

When Noel returned with the jack to the Lemon Mobile, Merrily was waiting, flanked by two rows of the

Deep River High School. Tyler ran to Mr. Tanner; a moment later the very nice man who'd happily bragged about his kids' silver medal finish with her song while he and Noel were changing the tire pulled out his phone and began to record.

Merrily waved at Noel, took a breath. And burst into "Grandma Got Run Over By a Reindeer". She sang melody on the first verse. A tall, muscular girl belted out the second verse with the power of a diva before Merrily sang the third. The entire choir joined on the choruses.

The driver of the white Nissan at the other pump and the cashier in the mini mart doorway all burst into applause when they were done. They looked absolutely thrilled about their semi-private concert, but Noel's reaction was the only one she really cared about.

"Let me know when you post it," Merrily said to Mr. Tanner. "I'll share it on my social media too. Tagging the choir, of course."

They took a bunch of selfies with each other with a backdrop of snow-covered trees and a single string of scrawny Christmas lights inside the mini mart's windows. But the atmosphere was more festive than Merrily had seen in some malls that were bursting with decorations and had piped in carols since the beginning of November. If anyone asked for an example of holiday magic, she had the perfect answer. She picked the clearest photo and uploaded it: ***TFW you have to burst into song along the TransCanada. #SomewhereOnHighway17 #DeepRiverHighSchoolChoir #RoadsideConcert #ChristmasEveMusic.***

"Thanks for this. The kids are playing it cool, but they are pretty pumped about it," the choir director said as he loaded his students back into the van.

"It was my pleasure," she assured him.

It was four thirty, with four hours to Ottawa. Another two to get to Montreal. She was running out of time with Noel. At least she'd been able to give him a Christmas present of sorts.

"That's my favourite Christmas carol," Noel said once they were on his way again.

Merrily grinned. "I know. Merry Christmas, Noel."

CHAPTER 10

THEY ARRIVED in Pembroke at six o'clock, almost an hour and a half behind schedule. The latest snowstorm was not letting up at all. Noel's excitement about Merrily's plan to get home half a day early on Christmas Eve was quickly fading. At this point he'd be lucky to make it there by his original deadline. They were so close to the finish line that he could practically taste it, but Mother Nature was throwing up every obstacle she could come up with to block their Christmas celebrations.

They were waiting for the bill at yet another truck stop diner. He was going to kiss his mom's feet when he got home and had a meal that didn't come off a griddle. Suddenly Merrily's attention switched from him to something happening behind him. A second later, she snatched his coffee cup from the table. "Incoming over your right shoulder!" she called as a boy scrambled over the seat back from the neighbouring booth.

Noel caught him before he fell, with the only damage being a set of napkin-wrapped silverware getting kicked to the floor when an errant boot scooted across the table-top. The boy giggled. His mother shrieked.

"Easton Grady, what do you think you're doing. Sit down this minute!" the dark-haired woman said. Stress etched every line on her face as she tried to wrangle the little boy, plus two girls who were around seven and eight years old. "I am so sorry. We left Timmins last night at ten o'clock with them asleep in the car. We were supposed to be in Ottawa before they woke up but the weather... And now they're awake and I need them to sit still for two more hours."

"No worries. No harm done," Noel assured her.

"The weather's a beast today," Merrily agreed. "We're behind schedule too. The good news is that the radar says we're reaching the end of the storm system. We should be in the clear now."

"Mom, I don't want to go to Grandpa's. Santa won't know where we are," the younger girl whined, interrupting their conversation.

"He'll know. I sent him an email."

"Of course he'll be able to find you. He's got GPS in his sleigh," Merrily said.

Noel smiled. It was official: Merrily was one of those people who had never met a stranger. She made a special effort with kids, like this one, acknowledging the little girl's worries.

He knew that travelling over the holidays was rough with lots of unfamiliar people and places and food. It was even harder for kids; they needed assurance that some things weren't going to change. "Everything in the North Pole is computerized, you know. If your Mom emailed Santa, he knows where you'll be because he has his Gift Positioning System telling him where to drop all his packages. Plus, there's a computer help line and people he can email if he has any questions."

Disbelieving eyes stared back at him. "No way."

"Trust me. I work for the North Pole," he said.

Across the table, Merrily's eyes got comically big. "Noel, what are you doing?"

"Trust me." Noel turned back to Easton's mom. "Let me give you one of my business cards." He was never going to have such a perfect opening again and he intended to take full advantage of the situation. He fumbled around until he pulled a small white card from his wallet. He handed it over to the kids' mom.

The woman gasped. "I'm Olivia Grady. These are my kids, Lily, Avery, and you've already met Easton. Lily, do you know what IT–information technology—is?"

"It's what Daddy does at work. He does computers for the company."

"Well, this is Mr. Noel Spouse, and he does IT too. This is the company he works for."

When Mrs. Grady passed her daughter the card, the other kids crowded around her. "What does it say?" Easton asked.

"Noel Sprouse. IT Specialist." Then her eyes got wide. "North Pole Unlimited. You work for the North Pole?" Lily demanded.

"I do."

"How come it says the North Pole is in Manitoba?"

"The computer department needed to be close to a big city. For repairs and stuff," Noel said as he retrieved his card. "I have my computer with me while I'm away from my office, plus a bunch of other people work there, too. If your mom told you that she emailed Santa to update your address, you'll all set."

Olivia Grady nodded that she had. Avery, the middle child, had gone very still. "Do you really work for the North Pole?"

Noel nodded.

"Okay."

"I think our work here is done," Merrily said.

"I cannot thank you enough for the next three hours of peace," Mrs. Grady said quietly as the kids huddled around two plates of pancakes to discuss this Christmas computer bombshell.

"It was my absolute pleasure," Noel said.

Merrily couldn't stop grinning as they started down the highway again, behind the Gradys' minivan. "That might be the single most impressive thing I've seen in years."

"Don't be funny."

"I'm serious," she argued. "Do you have any idea how popular those kids will be when they get back to school and tell their friends that they met Santa's IT guy? You have achieved legendary North Pole status, Noel! You have no idea how impressed I am with you. You made their Christmas Eve. I think you're amazing."

The look in her eyes when she glanced at him made his mild embarrassment at his actions a little more tolerable. It wasn't that Merrily was easy to please. She just recognized that the simple things had the biggest impact.

Noel sighed deeply, although it was edged with good humour. "Are we there yet?"

"Two hours to Ottawa, and then two more to Montreal. You'll be home this afternoon. What a story you'll have when you get there about your cross-Canada ordeal."

"I can't believe our road trip is almost over." His time

with her was coming to an end, but he wasn't willing to say so. In the new year, he'd be in December, and she'd be back in Vancouver. Technically, that wasn't so far away. In the summer they could drive it in two days.

He'd have other opportunities to see her again. He might have another conference, or she could come to North Pole Unlimited for business purposes. She might have problems with her digital contracts, the kind of problem that meant he'd have to see her in person.

He could make it happen.

But first he had to ask if she wanted it to.

CHAPTER 11

MERRILY COULDN'T CONTAIN her enthusiasm. The uncontrollable grin on her face made her cheeks hurt. This was her home turf, her old stomping grounds. She had camped a ton as a kid in the Arnprior area and felt obligated to point out to Noel every place that sold ice-cream as they drove along the scenic highway. Now that the snow had stopped falling and the wind had calmed, glimpses of the gorgeous Ottawa River appeared around turns in the highway before it vanished again.

She dialled up her focus as they approached the capital, not willing to risk an accident so close to the finish line. She stopped bouncing in her seat and concentrated fiercely on the roads and other vehicles until they turned off a main artery onto a quiet residential street. A couple of turns later, she pulled into the driveway of bungalow with a string of coloured lights along the eaves and a Christmas tree in the living room's picture window. "Home! I'm home!"

The side door to the van flew open, and Merrily loaded Noel down with bags and boxes, while she dragged a massive suitcase across the shovelled sidewalk to the front door. "Come on. Dad, Jenny, we're here!"

"Hello, Merrily. Merry Christmas!" An older, bald man with rounded shoulders waved from the porch next door. "You made it home after all."

"It's a story that best goes with cocoa, Mr. Farmington. We'll get together in a few days so I can regale you with my latest adventures. I know you're going to be a very busy man tonight," she replied.

"Honestly, do you know everybody?" Noel asked as she fumbled with her keys.

"That's Mr. Farmington. He's been our neighbour forever. He's one of Santa's helpers and is very busy on Christmas Eve, ensuring all the local kids know to keep on their best behaviour for at least one more night."

Noel nodded in understanding. "How lucky for the neighbourhood."

"Oh yes. My parents were thrilled that they weren't the ones doing all the reminding. We listened to Mr. Farmington better then did to them. He must be ready to hand over the tradition to the next generation soon. I'll ask him more about it later. For now, let's warm up for real."

The split-level house smelled of fresh-cut pine and cookies. Noel surveyed her parents' living room with undisguised interest. "It's been years since I've seen an upright piano! Most people switched over to electronic keyboards decades ago."

She tried to look around through his eyes. Her dad and stepmom were holding the piano for her until she had a place of her own. The piano's flat top was covered in picture frames, a handful of Christmas cards, and a dusty metronome. She had a small keyboard in her rented room because the compact instrument made sense in the tiny space, but she always considered it a poor substitute for the real thing.

It didn't look too out of place. The rest of the living room was decorated with an overstuffed sofa set, wooden coffee and end tables, and a flat screen television that dominated one wall. The Christmas tree in the window was impressive. It was a real Scotch pine with long green needles. Every ornament on it was red, or had red in it, from the flat felt ones to the shiny painted ceramic balls. White lights illuminated the whole thing.

"Hello, Lee-Lee darling. Is this Noel?" the only other occupant in the room said. He had short, white hair and looked like he was on the uncomfortable side of thin, with brown slacks and a brown, knit sweater. He stepped forward, hand out. "Merry Christmas, Noel. I hope you'll be able to stay for lunch. After five days in the Lemon-Mobile with my daughter, I'm sure you have some stories to share."

"Lunch would be great, Mr. Sweet. I contacted my folks once we knew when we'd be arriving in Ottawa, so they should be on their way," Noel said.

They had pulled into a gas station about half an hour outside the city. Topped up on gas, coffee and snacks, they hadn't needed to stop except for the fact that Merrily wanted to give Noel some privacy when he called his family. She didn't want to be within earshot if they made another crack about him not getting back to Montreal before Christmas like he promised after all he'd done for the last five days to be home for the holidays. When she came back with an unnecessary chocolate bar for each of them, he gave her a thumbs-up. "My parents were waiting for the call. They're leaving in ten minutes to drive to

Ottawa to pick me up. I'm supposed to text them with your address once we get there."

When Noel stepped away to update his parents, her dad sidled up to her. "He seems nice. How did you two meet?"

"That is the start of a very long story," Merrily said.

"We should have an hour before Noel's parents get here. We have time," her dad said.

They were carrying a plateful of grilled cheese sandwiches and bowls of tomato soup to the table when Noel came into the room, frowning at the phone in his hand. "Merrily, I don't think I can stay for lunch after all. I need to call an Uber to take me to the train station."

"Are your parents meeting you there instead?" It seemed like a waste of time to her. The Sweets' house was on the edge of the city; they'd have to drive farther to pick him up from the station. Unless... "Noel, are they still coming to pick you up?"

"I refuse to impose on you anymore, Merrily. It's Christmas Eve. You've done enough."

"What happened? I thought your parents had one foot out the door when you contacted them." Their son had travelled the better part of five thousand kilometres, through moose herds and snow and bitterly cold temperatures – surely, they could reach out for the last two hundred.

"They did. And when they had two feet out the door my mom hit a patch of ice and went down. They think she broke her foot. My dad had to drive her to the emergency room for X-rays. They're still at the hospital."

Noel's Christmas was cursed. It was the only logical explanation. "Oh, that sucks. If they aren't coming to get you, why do you want to go to the train station?" Then the truth behind Noel's request hit her like a snowball to the side of the head. "Have you lost your mind? Do you really think that you're going to be able to get a last-minute ticket home at noon on Christmas eve?" He'd be stuck there for hours, if not days, and she knew he'd never complain about it.

"I'm out of options, Merrily."

"I'm standing right here, Noel!"

Noel looked at her dad with fear in his eyes before his attention returned to her. "You finally made it home for Christmas. I'm not going to ask you for another four hours. You'd barely make it back in time for dinner."

"We eat late, don't we, Dad?"

"Eat your soup before it gets cold. We'll have a game plan for you by the end of lunch, Noel," her dad said.

Her father was not happy; Merrily could tell. It was really his own fault, teaching her all her life not to leave a job half-finished and not to ignore someone in need when she could help. When she looked at him again, he offered her a rueful smile, knowing she was going to do what she had to do.

"I can't let you drive me all the way to Montreal," Noel insisted.

She couldn't force him into the Lemon-Mobile. She also couldn't force him to stay. He'd been talking about seeing his family for days. His whole family. Which gave her an idea. "Where do your aunts live?" Merrily asked. "The ones who love Christmas. Are they in Montreal too?"

Noel was slow to respond. "Yes, actually."

"Would they be willing to meet us halfway?"

"I can ask."

Noel excused himself from the table, leaving Merrily with her dad.

"Five days of inescapable company and you're willing to get back into a car with him? He must be a special guy."

"He is, Dad. I like him."

"Is it leading anywhere?"

"Besides halfway to Montreal?" she joked. "We haven't discussed it, but I wouldn't object." What was a couple thousand kilometres between friends? Maybe it would go somewhere and maybe it wouldn't, but she was willing to take the chance. Even a freshly broken heart might give her some inspiration for a new song. Of course, a new love would be a lot more fun.

"It's a big risk, leaving town on Christmas Eve. With the traffic, I don't know if you'll make it back in time for supper and the evening carol service. But you can't abandon Noel at the train station either."

Noel returned wearing a hopeful expression. "How would you feel about a quick trip out to Hawkesbury?"

Merrily knew Hawkesbury. It was about halfway between Ottawa and Montreal on the Ontario side of the Ottawa River, about an hour away. If it was all the time she had left with Noel, she'd take it. "I think you should tell them to start driving in about twenty minutes to give you time to finish lunch."

CHAPTER 12

NOEL HAD TRAVELLED this highway too many times to count throughout his life, but never with a more attractive driver. For the first time in ages, he was the passenger and was able to get a good look at the various Christmas decorations on the rural properties they passed. He took a moment to appreciate and admire the efforts in the small towns they drove through.

Some houses were draped with the dripping light-icicles that were so popular twenty years ago. Others were carefully outlined with colourful LED-lights around the eavestroughs and windows. Some had the giant inflatables with six-foot Santas and eight-foot reindeers and cartoon characters decked out in wreath hats and ugly Christmas sweaters. He felt the anticipation of seeing his parents' home and the decorations of his childhood grow with every minute.

"Noel, what do you hope Santa leaves for you under the tree tonight?" Merrily asked after he pointed out a homestead where all the evergreens lining the drive were lit with hundreds of lights.

"An application for next year's ELF of the Year Innovation Award," he said.

She swerved a little on the road. "Really?" Her voice was an octave higher than normal. "You're going to do it? What happened?"

"I've been mainlining positivity and encouragement for the last five days. I'm ready to try." He left out the part about being terrified. He wanted to enjoy the look of sheer pride on Merrily's face when she looked at him.

"They're going to love it!"

"What if they don't?"

"Then you do it yourself, and burst into Nick Klassen's office and say, 'I told you so' after your first hundred thousand downloads."

Her enthusiasm about his future success was intimidating. "One hundred thousand downloads is a lot."

Merrily nodded. "Okay. Give them an 'I told you so' at ten thousand, and bring yourself caviar and champagne for lunch when you hit a hundred thousand," she countered. "You can invite him if you want but give him broken crackers with his caviar."

She never failed to make him laugh and anticipate the best. "That's a deal. How about you? What do you hope to find in your stocking on Christmas morning?"

"An orange in the toe, a new cozy mystery paperback, and a bottle of inspiration. Or at the very least, a workable song idea with a catchy chorus. Do you think Santa could whip that up in his workshop by tonight?"

"I think you're doing it on your own already," Noel said. He hadn't breathed a word about the fact that Merrily had been singing under her breath since her serenade at the gas station. She might not realize that she'd already come up with a chorus, but he'd memorized the eight-line refrain.

"I'm close. I can feel it. If I can get one song written, I know I could do more. I just need to finish the first one and get over the block."

Noel wanted so badly for Merrily to finish her song and get some of her amazing confidence working for herself. "That might be harder to wrap than the paperback."

"Come on, you're the Man in Red's number one IT guy. Don't you know somebody who knows somebody who can slip it onto his sleigh for me?"

"I'll see what I can do." He pointed to a gas station in the distance. "That's the place."

That was it. The end of the line. The grand finale of Noel and Merrily's Christmas Road Trip Adventure. The worst goodbye ever.

A green Beetle was parked in the corner of the lot, and two women got out and began waving madly as the Lemon-Mobile slowed to a stop. "I'm assuming that's them?" Merrily asked.

"If you want to see what my mom looks like, look no further than at the woman in the navy jacket. That's my aunt Iris, and she and my mom are identical twins. The lady in red is my aunt Mandy. It's their anniversary today, so I owe them huge for picking me up."

The twin aunt got to them first. "Noel, you made it. Your mom is going to be thrilled. Your father just texted. She's third on the list barring emergencies to see a doctor." The blond whirlwind spun to face Merrily. "And you must be Merrily. Thanks for getting my favourite nephew home for Christmas. Especially since it took you away from your own family. We really appreciate it."

"It was my pleasure. I'm glad to meet you, Iris. Noel talked about you a lot. He was excited about how excited you'd be for Christmas." She considered hinting about Noel's app, but that was a step too far, especially since he'd originally designed it as a present for this very aunt.

"That's sweet. We've missed this little rug rat too."

"Iris!"

"Well, you were. And now you're my adorable grown-up nephew. Who needs to be at home waiting when your mother gets back, or she'll never let any of us hear the end of it."

"Give us a minute to say goodbye?"

His aunt looked from him to Merrily and back again. "We'll wait in the car. You'll have to fold yourself into the back seat but we left the dog at home so you should have enough room. Don't be too long."

The sound of traffic roaring by on the highway, the scent of diesel exhaust in the air, and the fact that he hadn't had a warm shower in two days didn't make it the most romantic setting in the world, but it was what he had. Noel hoped that what he said would make up for it. He reached for Merrily's mittened hand. "This has been the most unexpected, unusual, unforgettable Christmas of my life. I'm very sorry it has to end."

"Me, too."

This was the tricky part. "I'm not ready for it to be over. How long are you going to be in Ottawa?" he asked. He didn't know if they'd have a chance to see each other again, but he was willing to make the effort.

"Until New Year's Day, give or take a couple of days. Then I'll be driving back to Vancouver."

There was the opportunity he was looking for. "So you'll be driving back through Manitoba?"

"I have to if I want to keep my wheels on the ground."

"And it's necessary for you to take rest breaks, right?"

Her eyes lit up as she caught on. "Well, that would be the safe, responsible thing to do."

"And maybe you'd want a co-pilot for part of the trip? If, for instance, you arrived on a Friday night, a person could help you navigate the trip west for two days and fly home on Sunday night on an airline credit and still be at work on time on Monday morning."

"If it was properly planned, they sure could."

"Are you planning to arrive in Winnipeg on a Friday night?" Noel asked hopefully.

"I am now."

"Then it's a date. Our first *official* date," he corrected. He'd wanted to ask her five minutes after they met but it had taken him five thousand kilometres. But he finally got his yes.

The green Beetle honked at them. "I really should go."

"Merry Christmas, Noel."

"Merry Christmas, Merrily."

He made it as far as the car door. "Nope, can't do it," he said to himself. Then he spun on his heel and sprinted back to the Lemon-Mobile. Merrily looked up to him, her blue eyes full of questions, which he answered with one swift, heartfelt, holiday kiss.

"Now it's a merry Christmas, Merrily Sweet."

She grinned at him. "If that was Christmas, I can't wait until New Year's."

EPILOGUE

NOEL'S HANDS were soft against her cold, clammy ones as he rubbed her fingers to warm them before Merrily stepped onto the stage at the Diamond Willow Festival in Hopewell, Manitoba. The hot August sun beat down on the street behind the bandstand, making her sweat more.

"Stop panicking, Merrily. You've got this," her boyfriend of eight months said reassuringly.

Things between her and Noel had moved pretty quickly since Christmas. Noel had been as good as his word after the holidays. Merrily had arrived in Manitoba on a Friday night in early January. Noel played navigator all day Saturday until they arrived in Calgary that night, and then they had a shorter day on Sunday to drive the rest of the way to Vancouver, ending up at the airport for Noel to fly home that evening to be back at work for Monday.

It had been the best trip of her life—even better than Christmas. A few more weekend visits had made it clear where Merrily's heart and inspiration laid, so she'd moved to Winnipeg as soon as her lease was up. Considering that she finished writing and recording her first new album in years within a month of making the move, she was certain she'd made the right choice.

Now she wasn't so sure. "That's sweet, but I think I'm going to throw up."

"About this little crowd? No way."

"This crowd isn't so little." She'd taken a shot in the dark when she'd applied to play at the Diamond Willow Festival, one of the larger country fairs in Manitoba. After first ending up on the wait list, a time slot had become available that fit into her schedule. Merrily was thrilled to get a spot on the same day as new country star Tyler Lawson, who was headlining the Saturday night show. Fans of his had arrived early to make sure they had a good view of the stage, and every other performer was enjoying the benefits.

"What's different about it?" Noel asked.

"For starters, it will be the first time I'll be singing a love song when the guy I'm singing about will be in the audience," Merrily said. It wasn't the first time she'd said the words, but they always gave her a thrill. She'd lived a big life before Noel came upon the scene, but she'd never had bigger feelings than the ones she'd had for him.

"You know I love you, too." Noel kissed her sweetly but thoroughly, considering their current location. He did a good job; she appreciated that he was a very good kisser. She really appreciated that she could enjoy more of them now that they only lived thirty minutes apart.

But it didn't solve all her problems. "Thank you, but I still want to throw up." She'd just received notification that "Ride", her second song off her new album, had cracked the top hundred on the charts at a precarious number ninety-eight. She was singing it in her set.

Cracking the top one hundred was an event in itself for her. What happened next would tell her whether or not people were ready to welcome Merrily Sweet back to the music world.

"I promise you that you've got this. Get ready for your introduction, take that stage by storm, and play your heart out. I have to go grab my seat. I don't want to miss seeing you play."

"How did you save yourself a seat? It's rush seating."

"Nick Klassen made an extraordinary donation to the Hopewell Tornado Rebuilding Fund and managed to reserve an entire row in front of the stage for your concert."

Merrily dropped her face into her hands. "Or he could have, you know, asked me to block a row for him."

"But this way he can prove that he's still your number one fan," Noel told her with a laugh. "You know, he's still claiming that he's the one who got us together. Like he arranged the moose on the runway or something."

"Stranger things have happened at North Pole Unlimited," Merrily said. Since she started showing up there more often to work with the marketing department and visiting Noel, she'd heard stories. A lot of them.

"He might be your biggest fan, but I love you more. Now go impress this crowd."

Noel was the best. Before he could vanish, she grabbed his arm. "Wait. What's the Christmas Every Day task for today? Maybe I can get extra points for doing it on stage."

"Can't you look it up?"

"You have my phone." She'd given it to him after posting a pre-concert picture. ***About to hit the stage*** *at #DiamondWillowFestival #RockOn #Ride-ToTheTopOfTheCharts.*

Noel sighed and called up the app that his bosses had jumped on back in January. It had taken them less than two weeks to make an offer after he'd made his presentation. "Make sure you say the words to somebody you love," he read aloud.

Merrily smiled and kissed him again. "I already did."

THE END

If you enjoyed this book, sign up for Elle's newsletter and keep up to date about upcoming releases and other events.

RECIPE: GRINCH COOKIES

If you are like Merrily and don't have time to bake this year, consider modifying some store-bought cookie dough into festive Grinch cookies (or make them from scratch.)

½ cup butter
¼ to ½ tsp mint extract
6-8 drops of green food colouring
1 egg
1 package Betty Crocker sugar cookie mix (or other packaged mix)**
1 cup chocolate chips

Combine the egg, butter, mint extract and green food colouring.

Then add the sugar cookie mix and stir thoroughly until it is all evenly green. (Do not add the food colouring after the cookie mix because the colouring will be spotted and uneven.)

Add chocolate chips.

Put on a non-stick pan. Cook at 350F for 8-10 minutes.

Homemade Grinch Sugar Cookie Recipe

If you don't want to buy a packaged sugar cookie mix, you can easily make this recipe from scratch.

1 cup butter, softened
1 egg
½ teaspoon vanilla extract
¼ to ½ teaspoon mint extract
6-8 drops of green food colouring

1 ½ cups white sugar
2¾ cups all-purpose flour
1 teaspoon baking soda
½ teaspoon baking powder
1 cup chocolate chips

Combine the egg, butter, vanilla extract, mint extract, and green food colouring.

Then add the sugar, flour, baking soda, and baking powder. Stir thoroughly until it is all evenly green. (Do not add the food colouring after the dry ingredients because the colouring will be spotted and uneven.)

Add chocolate chips.

Put on a non-stick pan. Cook at 350F for 8-10 minutes.

JACK AND BELLE

A North Pole Unlimited Sweet Christmas Romance
by
Elle Rush

Belle Silver can't artistically express her love of all things Christmas. Her disastrous baking brings all the fire-fighters to the yard. She won't even talk about her choir audition. But she refuses to lose December's annual holiday decorating contest to her nemesis and next-door-neighbour.

Ever since Jack Foster started at North Pole Unlim-ited, he's won every Christmas design accolade there but one - the December Light Spectacular trophy. The only obstacle in his path to victory will be Belle's unique and unpredictably themed yard.

Sabotage is the name of the game for these competi-tors, until they are forced to play nice at work when they draw each other's names in the office's Secret Santa exchange. It's going to take a friend in need and some serious Christmas magic for this pair to put down the snowballs and find a spot under the mistletoe.

PROLOGUE

SATURDAY, *November 26*

Jilly Lewis-Fredericks and Ginger Cardinal were at the High Five—December's budget-friendly "Nothing is priced higher than five dollars" store—on a mission to get a basketful of baby shower decorations before everything in the store was replaced with Christmas decor. They were almost too late. They had to squeeze down rows clogged with their coworkers on the hunt for cheap winter decorations and detour around mobs of children looking for holiday craft supplies. So far, they'd found purple and pink crepe streamers and matching plates, but the coordinating napkins eluded them.

Ginger volunteered to check the tissue paper and giftwrap aisle while Jilly headed to housewares in the slim hopes that they'd find a pack that had been mis-shelved.

They didn't find any napkins, but Jilly did spy something else. Something that interested her *tremendously*.

Belle Silver had her booted toes on the base of a rack

and was holding on for dear life as she stretched her arm along the top shelf, reaching for something out of sight.

"Nuts," Belle said as she came away emptyhanded.

Jilly had no clue what should be on that particular shelf. It was as bare as a chocolate display at six o'clock on Valentine's Day. Belle gripped the edge of the metal rack and pulled herself on to her tiptoes to see if any loose packets had been pushed to the back. Her groan indicated she was out of luck.

Jilly liked Belle. She was friendly in person, but her work emails were short and concise. With the volume of correspondence that Jilly handled for the VP of Human Resources, short was always better. "What are you looking for, Belle? More replacement baking pans? Maybe I can help." She crossed her fingers and hoped Belle wasn't experiencing a replay of the previous year, when the volunteer fire department had made a house call to her place in what was now referred to locally as "the Silver event."

Belle looked down and smiled, since she was half a foot taller than Jilly, and that was before taking the extra shelf height into account. "I'm looking for zip ties."

"What size?"

"Any!"

Jilly took another look down the aisle. Belle was right. Every single zip-tie was gone. Not just the large ones. Or the extra-large ones. All of them, even the mostly useless two-inch ones that could barely keep a computer cord bundled together.

Belle waved down a teenage stockboy wearing a nametag that said "Ryder. "Excuse me. Do you have any more zip-ties in the back?"

"No, sorry," he said.

Belle huffed, and Jilly began to get an inkling of how serious the situation was. The unflappable temperament of the head of North Pole Unlimited's Special Projects Unit was legendary. "Could you please check?" Belle requested.

"I just did. The guy at the till bought every single pack we have in stock. But Mr. Marsh puts in orders every Friday, so we should be restocked in a week or two," Ryder told her.

Belle's eyes shot to the checkout counter and Jilly watched her turn beet red.

"I can't tell who that is," Jilly said, staring hard at the back of a woodland green ski jacket trimmed with navy piping.

"Mr. Anti-Christmas Spirit himself. The most devious person in all of December. Trouble in a toque."

That was some first-rate annoyance there, Jilly thought. "He sounds terrible. What's the miscreant's name?"

"Jack Foster. My next-door neighbour." When Belle started marching toward the counter, Jilly texted Ginger to meet her in housewares *immediately*.

Jilly knew that Jack Foster had an impeccable reputation as the head of the marketing department. He was a Yuletide perfectionist, especially when it came to his designs and displays for the holidays. He was so good at capturing the essence of the season that he had a shelf full of awards. Not one of them used the words "anti-Christmas".

Belle stood right beside Jack, blocking him from moving to the exit. "Jack, buddy, could you possibly spare me any of those zip-ties?"

Jack shook his head sadly, his sandy brown locks

brushing his forehead. "Sorry, my bestie Belle. They're vital components to a very special project for the community. You know how it is."

"Interesting," Jilly whispered to herself. When Ginger appeared at her side, Jilly nudged her with her elbow and pointed at the unfolding scene at the register.

Everybody in December knew about the rivalry between Belle and Jack when it came to decorating their homes for the December Light Spectacular. Jack had thousands of lights, and a two-storey house as a canvas. Belle, on the other hand, tended to stick more to yard decorations that had an interactive component.

The competition didn't surprise Jilly. What shocked her was the undercurrent running between the pair.

"How about one package? You must have twenty there," Belle said.

"Sorry, they're all spoken for."

Belle muttered under her breath.

"I didn't catch what she said," Jilly said quietly.

"I hope your hydro bill bankrupts you," Ginger responded, her eyes wide with excitement. When Jilly looked at her, she shrugged. "What? I can read lips."

"What was that?" Jack asked.

"I sure hope all those zip-ties are for holding LED lights in place. I wouldn't want your Christmas decorating budget to go to break the bank with electricity costs."

"That's awfully sweet of you, Belle. Rest assured, they are LEDs. I'm sure you'll find some zip-ties somewhere else."

Jilly snorted. Like Belle had oodles of spare time to drive around southern Manitoba looking for fasteners to keep her bulbs in a picture-perfect position. "Thanks, anyways, pal," Belle said before she walked away.

"He's going to pay for that," Ginger noted. She wasn't wrong.

"Come along, my little protégé. We have work to do," Jilly ordered. It was a good thing that her capacity for giving was endless at this time of year.

1. BELLE

The reception area of North Pole Unlimited's Special Projects Unit looked like it had been professionally decorated for Christmas, and for good reason. It had been. Belle Silver had scoured the internet looking for the best of the best when it came to holiday décor. She'd then forwarded her vision board to an interior designing friend with instructions to replicate them with a massive budget, provided by Belle personally.

Now, with only four weeks left till Christmas, Belle looked around in satisfaction. The little vignettes around the reception area—the miniature winter village atop the credenza nestled in a sea of white cotton snow, the quartet of perfectly framed antique Christmas cards hanging on the wall, plus the five-foot pencil-thin, pre-lit tree loaded with silver and mauve ornaments in the corner of the conference room—all flawlessly proclaimed that Belle was participating in the season in the most perfect way possible.

It wasn't that she *wanted* to hire a designer to take care of the task. She didn't have a choice. Belle needed to outsource it because she was horrible at Christmas decorating. Abysmal. So unbelievably bad that she made Ebenezer Scrooge's non-existent holiday stylings looked good.

It wasn't her fault. Belle loved Christmas. It was her favourite holiday. And she loved her job at North Pole Unlimited. She had been a fan and customer of the world's best Christmas company since she was a little kid. Getting a job with them had been like winning the lottery because she got to work in a place where it was Christmas every day of the year. She couldn't ask for more.

Except for her health insurance to cover the surgery she desperately needed to graft the gene that would make her good at decorating for the holidays into her DNA. Or the gene responsible for succeeding at Christmas crafts. Or the one for baking. Because while her spirit was willing...

Belle grimaced then laughed as she took in the tiny, self-decorated corner of her private office where she had tried to Christmas-fy her collection of coffee pod stands. Her inspiration pictures resembled a trio of mini trees. The green garland that she'd threaded through the chrome loops made hers look like a particularly nasty mold infestation. She'd tried. She really had. But there was a reason that her trusted administrative assistant was the only person usually allowed in her office. That, and the fact that her coffee pod collection was company-renown and was prone to disappear if left unguarded.

Speaking of her coffee-loving assistant, Grace appeared in her doorway. "I'm heading out. Jack Foster's new notes for the Christmastown marketing proposal have been loaded to the server. And Noel from IT messaged to say that he was on his way up. Is there a problem?" the green-haired woman asked.

"I had a question that I couldn't explain in writing, so I wanted to show him on my computer in person," Belle lied. "You go. I'll see you in the morning."

"Knit Night tonight?"

Belle nodded. "I'm almost finished the baby hat. It's a lot better than the last one."

"Good for you!" Grace said loyally. She'd seen Belle working on it diligently over her lunch hours. While it was made with a great deal of love, Belle's skill level meant it was never going to be mistaken as a professionally knit one. "See you in the morning."

Belle's knitting class was supposed to be a peaceful, creative endeavour that she enjoyed once a week. But right now, she had to wage a little war. She already had to drive to Winnipeg for her knitting lessons. That meant that she wasn't exactly put out if she had to make an extra stop to buy more zip-ties.

It was the principle of the matter. Jack Foster needed some payback, and she was about to deliver. Since the company's newest computer guru owed her one, what she had in mind would give Noel a chance to return a favour and her a chance to teach Jack a lesson. Everybody would win.

"Noel, my friend, come in. Can I offer you a coffee?"

Belle offered. She wasn't expecting him to make a teeny-tiny programming change completely for free.

"Do you have any of those famous vanilla latte pods?" Noel Sprouse asked.

"Of course."

"Fantastic. What can I do for you?" he asked while she set a visitor's mug in the coffee maker.

"There's a slight correction I'd like you to make on one of the North Pole Unlimited Christmas playlists," Belle said. She loved that the company had put together several playlists for their employees on their internal servers. They had religious songs, secular popular music, novelty songs for kids, one playlist of orchestral music, and another playlist of Christmas audio books. They even had one for their own holiday albums. Since Belle's first special project at the company had been to establish their recording division, that one was her favourite.

"Is there a problem?"

"It needs a little tweak to one title," she assured him. She pointed at the playlist she'd already displayed on the monitor. "This song. I need it to say, "Dedicated to Jack Foster.""

Noel blinked. "You want this song title to read, "Dedicated to Jack Foster" instead of "You're a Mean One, Mr. Grinch." Do I have that right?"

"It's on the company's internal intranet. Nobody outside the office will see it. I only need it to appear for a couple days until somebody gets the message."

"Is this about the zip-ties?" he asked.

She'd seen Noel in the High Five; he knew what Jack had done. "It's not *not* about the zip-ties. I prefer to think of it as a friendly reminder of the importance of being neighbourly at this time of year."

Noel shook his head. He did it laughing, though.

"I doubt that Jack will even notice. If he complains, switch it back to the proper title and send him to my office. I can handle him," she promised.

"I don't know, Belle."

"You don't know if you can help me after I came in to work on a weekend—twice—to discuss your girlfriend's new contract so you two could spend your vacations together and not have to interrupt them for work? Noel, I'm shocked at you." She tried to keep a straight face. She would have come in at midnight to meet popstar Merrily Sweet, so the very apologetic request for a Saturday morning appointment hadn't been a hardship.

"Fine, but you're clearing it with Dave this afternoon," Noel relented. "Unless he vetoes it, it'll be done by tomorrow morning."

"You're a gem, Noel. Besides, you never know. Maybe dedications will be the next big thing," Belle said. She handed Noel a steaming latte.

"I'm out of here. I'll return your mug in the morning," he promised.

2. JACK

Belle Silver was in *his* parking spot. Jack Foster knew that North Pole Unlimited didn't have assigned spots, but the end space on the first row was large, close to the front door, and allowed for an almost straight-shot to the road to make a quick escape at the end of the day. Parking there was a perk of being the first one at the office.

Belle had taken it. Again. Since it was eight in the morning, and there was an inch of snow on the hood, she'd evidently been at work for some time already. She'd probably arrived early to find more ways to make his job harder. He and his team spent thousands of hours every year creating picture-perfect Christmas moments for North Pole Unlimited's online store. It took time to create the perfect campaign. It wasn't his fault that Belle kept shooting down all his ideas for the company's newest special project. It was hers; she didn't recognize genius when she saw it.

He was still grumbling when he walked through the front doors. He unzipped his coat in the lobby, revealing his Icelandic pullover with its blue and white snowflake design. He paused when Barb at the reception desk snickered when he walked by. Then two IT staffers saw him coming, waved, and darted into their offices before he could say hello. "What's going on with people today?" he asked Carolyn, a social media expert and the newest addition to his department.

"There's a new Christmas playlist that's getting lots of attention. An all-dedication list. It's on the internal servers."

"I'll look later. We have to hit the ground running. I have a meeting this morning with Belle Silver regarding the upcoming Christmastown project. I'm not looking forward to it. She hasn't been happy with anything we've presented. I have no idea what she wants."

Jack wasn't new to the position of Marketing Director, but this job did have additional challenges. Prior to starting with North Pole Unlimited, he was used to celebrating events six months in advance. This was his first experience where everything was Christmas all day, every day, all year. It was a unique opportunity, which was why he'd been willing to take a five-year contract.

But his time in December might be coming to an end. Professionally, he was concerned that he might be tapped out on Christmas ideas. He was afraid that five years of non-stop holiday advertising was the reason he couldn't come up with a winning idea for the Christmastown project. If he didn't have a breakthrough soon, he was going to have to admit defeat, something he had never done on a job before. He'd have to leave December in shame.

Personally, Jack wondered if he'd stayed in Manitoba too long already. His mother had been making noise about how nice it would be for him to return to Toronto, reminding him that he was missing seeing his brothers' and sister's kids grow up. Jack saw his nieces and nephews two or three times a year and never missed sending them birthday and Christmas presents. She had a point. Spending more time with his siblings and niblings would be fun.

"Don't forget that registration for the Secret Santa draw is happening in the cafeteria at noon," Carolyn told him.

He grinned in anticipation. Who didn't like getting gifts? "I'm in. Last year, Jilly was my Secret Santa. She gave me one of her imported cookies on the final day. It was worth the hype."

That reminder was the best part of his morning. The rest deteriorated into an exercise in frustration as he went head-to-head with his arch nemesis. He and his department were hosting the latest meeting regarding the newest North Pole Unlimited special project: Christmastown, an amusement park that was scheduled to open the next year. Hopefully being on his home turf would be lucky because none of the other meetings had gone his way. The worst part was that he couldn't even pull rank with Belle and say "Trust me" because this time, North Santana, the CEO of the entire company, was attending too.

North was just as tall, blonde, and Viking-like as the rest of her siblings. It was a Klassen-family trait. She also had the same stubbornness, which was not working in his favour. "You're not getting it, Jack. We need fun, not formal. Haven't you ever been to a theme park?"

"Sure. I went to Canada's Wonderland when I was a kid." It was practically mandatory for any child in Toronto to have gone at least once.

"Did you wear your good clothes so you could take some nice birthday pictures? Did your parents take you to a five-star restaurant for lunch in between rides?" Belle's sarcasm was as cutting as the marker she was taking to his mock-up ads. It was a shame that her bad attitude made it impossible for him to appreciate the cute dimple she had on her left cheek.

"Of course not."

"Then why are you showing me sit-down family dinners with kids and two generations of adults around a formal table? Christmastown will have a served buffet restaurant and a fast-food style diner. There's not going to be a tablecloth in sight!"

"We're trying to portray a feeling, Belle."

"Is that feeling "This park is for stuffed shirt adults"? Because that is the vibe I'm getting."

Jack bit his tongue. She was right. The images he'd provided were all of Christmas dinners with no kids or babies in sight.

Fortunately, North stepped in before things could deteriorate further. "Your marketing for North Pole Unlimited has won awards, Jack. We all know that. I also know that we've expanded significantly in the last few years and there is a lot to cover. Are we overloading your department? The website and catalogue sales will be funding Christmastown for the first few years, so we can't risk a drop in sales there. Do you think we should look for a separate team for this new division of the company?" North asked.

"No. My department can handle it." Jack understood

the reason behind North's question, but he was not going back to his people and telling them that the boss thought they were in over their heads.

"Okay, we'll try it again," North agreed. "But we need to have something locked down by the end of the year or I'll have to take it to an outside contractor, Jack. Work with Belle and see what you can do."

"Jack, please try to remember that Christmastown is going to be a live, outdoor, experience," Belle said for the millionth time. She pushed her black hair out of her face and leaned forward earnestly over the table. "We need to see fun. Show us activity with screaming, laughing kids and fresh air and real people in the snow."

He felt his hackles rise. "Okay. Here's something for the one-horse open sleigh ride." He opened his file of mock-ups for the romantic date night the park intended to offer: the horse and pristine sleigh, the driver in a dark, unobtrusive uniform, and a couple snuggled under a plaid blanket in the double seat behind him. It was picture-perfect.

"That is exactly what we want!" North exclaimed.

He smiled for the first time. Finally, she was coming around.

"What about the hayride?" the CEO continued.

"We've started on that," Jack hedged. "The problem is getting a bunch of children on a wagon smiling at the camera at the same time. It always looks like they're in a class photo."

"Why do they all have to be looking at the camera?" Belle asked.

"It's better visuals to see smiling, happy people."

"In a catalogue," Belle added. "But realistically, if you take a photo of a group of people on a hayride, you're going to get the back of one person's head, somebody laughing, and a kid mining for boogers."

North snort-laughed while he grimaced. "Is that what you want?" Jack asked.

"I could do without seeing that kid, but other than that, yes. Christmastown's primary promises are to be fun, family-friendly and accessible. We don't need perfect. We need happy and memorable."

Jack didn't get it. In his experience, no matter what they said, customers wanted perfectly preserved memories to display and show off to their friends. What Belle was describing was the type of photo people had on their phones. There was a difference. It was his job to make her see it. "I'll see what we can come up with."

Then he took his notes back to his team and managed not to choke when he repeated the suggestion for candid photographs. "If we were ever going to be inspired, this is the season for it. They want family friendly, so let's use that as a springboard to more ideas, okay, team?" Jack tried to sound upbeat, but he didn't know where to start. How could his well be running dry on holiday ideas after only a dozen years in the business?

"Maybe we need carbs," Carolyn suggested. "Should we break for lunch?"

Jack's stomach rumbled its agreement with the proposal, even though his brain said they needed to push through until they had a resolution. "Fine. Clear your schedules and we'll try again tomorrow morning. We need to come up with something perfect, people, so let those ideas simmer and I want everybody to bring something new and exciting to the table."

"Now, lunch!" Carolyn said happily as they all shuffled toward the door.

3. BELLE

Belle's calendar was strained to its limits. Her endless list of holiday commitments continued. First, she'd signed up for the office's Secret Santa at lunch. Now she was registering for the December Light Spectacular Decorating Contest. It was a rite of passage for Decemberites. Belle had never won, but this was her year. She'd been planning for months and had even assembled her design's framework in her front yard at the end of October before the first snow of the season. She was ready.

The doors finally swung open, and the crowd shuffled toward the folding table. Belle approached the first free volunteer.

"Name?" asked the woman sitting behind the table.

"Belle Silver. Belle with an "e" at the end," she specified, like her down-the-street neighbour Amanda didn't already know.

"Address?"

"142 Second Street."

"Residential or commercial?"

"Residential."

"Judging is set for December twenty-first, between six and nine. Any questions?"

"Yeah. Can I borrow Tim's two-storey ladder if I need it?" Belle asked. Amanda's husband had a shed full of useful tools he was happy to loan out.

"Of course! Sign here to acknowledge the rules and regulations."

Belle grabbed the offered pen and scrawled her signature at the bottom of the form. "Great. I'll text you after work tomorrow and set a time. Right now, I have to run." She was on the verge of being late to her knitting lesson.

The trip into Winnipeg took an hour. Belle snuck in with a minute to spare. She slipped into an empty space on the blue sofa at the front of Knots of Love just as her craft buddy returned to her seat with a new set of knitting needles.

"Did you finish it?" Carolyn Brown asked. The tall Jamaican Canadian had been her best friend forever, even after Carolyn's father had been transferred across the country when they were in the eighth grade. Five years later they'd reconnected at university and had been insep-arable ever since. Belle had thrown a party the previous spring when Carolyn had accepted a job in North Pole Unlimited's marketing department.

"Almost." Belle pulled the blue baby hat from her bag carefully, ensuring the little pink stoppers stayed firmly attached to the ends of her cable needle. "I need to decrease four more rows and I'll be done." Those four rows would take her most of the night, but it would be worth it to do it right.

Carolyn examined it carefully. "Belle, this is such an improvement over the last two! Who are you going to give it to?"

"I'm planning to give it to Joy at her baby shower. Her little Harkness will be able to wear it till spring. It's too bad that I didn't know she was having a girl when I started it."

"She'll love it." Carolyn would know. She and Joy both had kids in the North Pole Unlimited day care. "Are you ready for a new project?"

"What do you suggest?" Belle was at a loss. She liked knitting, but she didn't have the confidence for anything more challenging yet.

"Same hat. Adult sized this time. With..." Carolyn paused dramatically, "a stripe."

Belle gasped. Colour-work was an entirely different level. "Really? Do you think I'm ready?"

"Absolutely. It will help cement the pattern and techniques into your brain. You already know them. It would just be on a larger scale. I think you could finish it in a week or two and have another Christmas present ready to give."

Belle was gob-smacked. She'd been coming to Knit Night for over two years and the baby hat was the first thing she felt remotely comfortable giving to another person, mostly because a baby couldn't complain. If Carolyn thought she could produce a toque worthy of being a gift, Belle might finally have conquered her life-long inability to do crafts. "A whole adult hat? What colours would I use?" Belle's eye for colours was as terrible as her present-wrapping skills.

"A nice evergreen, maybe. With a blue stripe. You could use the left-over yarn from this project. It's a masculine pattern, and those will go with most men's jackets colours," Carolyn suggested.

"Are you sure I can do this?"

"Yes. If you don't like it, you can always frog it and try again another time."

Belle didn't want to fail at something else. She had a closet full of abandoned, misshapen, and ruined crafts. Her most recent attempt resulted in a quarter of a cross-stitched ornament that had ended in a tangle of all the coloured threads she was using and, somehow, an old shoelace. She was giving up hope on finding a creative endeavour on the planet that she could do without messing up.

It was a good thing she agreed to make the hat. She had time for it since she wasn't going to be baking.

That became obvious on Saturday when she arrived at the Winter Extravaganza Bake Sale meeting. The bake sale secretary reported how many people had already volunteered to donate to the baked goods table. Then she asked for anyone who wanted to make a donation but hadn't signed up yet to see her after the meeting.

Belle waited her turn before offering to add herself to the list. "I'll do Cocoa Puffed Wheat Squares," Belle offered. They were simple. Even better, she was successful half of the times she tried the recipe. If she goofed once or twice, she should still be able to make two or three trays to donate. The bags of puffed wheat at the grocery store were huge.

"That's very generous of you, Belle, but—"

"I was also considering doing bags of pre-made Nuts

and Bolts. It would be convenient for people if they could just fill a bowl rather than making it themselves," she continued. As long as she didn't forget to set the timer on the oven again, those were easy.

"Actually, we wanted to ask if you would act as treasurer for the entire bake sale and supervise the cash table," Helen Gauthier said. "I know we'd be taking advantage of your work experience, but we hoped you wouldn't mind."

Belle would have volunteered to help at the cash table anyway. There was no reason she couldn't drop off her goodies and then get to work except... "Is this about the gumdrop cake I donated last year? Because that was a new recipe. They guaranteed it was fool proof."

It was the first and only time she'd ever heard of something being returned to the bake sale for a full refund.

"We appreciate all of your donations. This year, though, we thought we'd seize the opportunity and ask you to get us organized before we ended up with the usual chaos. That's a job and a half. We couldn't ask you to do more on top of that."

That smarted. But not nearly as much as what she saw over Helen's shoulder. Belle saw another volunteer pull Jack into a hug. Then Belle heard her say, "Save a batch of your mother's chocolate covered shortbread for me. I had some last year, and it is divine!"

"You got it," Jack promised.

"Sure, I'll work the cash desk," Belle said to Helen. She wasn't gracious about it, but at least Helen had tried to spare her feelings.

Belle couldn't believe that they were begging Jack for Christmas baking, and she wasn't allowed to contribute anything. Jack's flawless Christmas reputation was stomach-turning. His totally not-ugly holiday sweaters. His awesome gift displays. And now his baking. He was Mr. Perfect Christmas himself.

But not this year. This Christmas, he was going down.

4. JACK

"Hi, Mr. Foster!" Jack peered over the snow pile at the foot of his driveway at Madison Hill from down the street, who was being taken for a walk by her Golden Retriever, Bucky. "Are you starting your decorating? What's the holiday design going to be this year?"

"You'll have to wait and see just like everybody else," Jack said. He wasn't giving any hints about this year's theme. "How about you?"

"We're having normal lights on the house. I think my mom is working on a new wreath for the front door, though. She registered for a workshop at North Pole Evergreens."

"Tell her to have a good time."

"Mom said that Miss Silver also registered for the decoration competition. Any idea as to what she's doing?" Madison asked.

"Nope, but I know it won't look as good as mine."

"That's the holiday spirit. I love a good Christmas light fight," the teenager cheered. "Don't get frostbite."

Jack had a detailed blueprint for his design. It started with a narrow path running from the side of his house across his front yard so he could run a set of extension cords. He grabbed his shovel, and the snow began to fly. As he cleared a path between his house and the towering, thirty foot evergreen that separated his house from his neighbour's, he noticed something he hadn't seen from the street.

Belle had cleared a huge square in the middle of her yard where her mysterious flagpole was, the one that she'd never hung a flag from. December hadn't had much snow yet, but she had a defined open space, with mounds of snow around the perimeter. No wonder why it looked like she had more snow than everybody else on the block. He couldn't believe she was so much further ahead of him, so he rolled his shoulders and started again with renewed vigour.

"Hey! Hey, stop!"

Jack heard the words. He didn't realize they were directed at him until the back of his head and neck were covered in snow. He whirled around to see Belle leaning on a shovel. "What is wrong with you?"

"Wrong with me? I'm not the one refilling a path that I shovelled by hand on my own property!" Belle leaned against her shovel, glaring daggers at him, while her red cheeks huffed clouds of indignant, frosty breath.

"What are you talking about?"

She gestured at the inside of her cleared square, which was now covered in a fresh layer of recently tossed snow. Jack didn't realize that he'd thrown it so far. "It's just a little snow, Belle. I didn't do it on purpose."

"On purpose or not, you can have it back." She took a shovelful of snow and threw it back over the property line. Right into his face.

Jack shivered as little clumps of snow fell between his scarf and his skin, then proceeded to run down his neck in ice-cold rivulets. "You know, the first time I did it was an accident. This is on purpose." He scooped a towering shovelful of snow and aimed it at the empty space three feet behind Belle. It wasn't his fault she was standing in the way.

The shovel quickly got in his way, so he abandoned it. The snow was too cold and crystalized to pack properly, so his snowballs were mostly handfuls of powder that disintegrated as soon as they left his mittened hands. Belle fared no better with her ammunition.

"What are you two lunatics doing? Didn't you read the rules? Do you both want to be disqualified from the December Light Spectacular?" Jack was grateful for the break when they both turned to see who as addressing them. Amanda Hill, Madison's mother, had carried her grocery bags down the street from her car to chastise them.

More than the cold, Amanda's words stopped him dead in his tracks. "What?"

"Section two, subsection two requires all decorators to stick strictly to their own property. Section four, subsection two is about not assaulting fellow competitors or judges," Amanda quoted. "Generally, we only have to quote that one when it comes to children getting rowdy when they are competing against their next-door-neighbours, but apparently hooliganism doesn't have an age limit. Really, you two! Does "Peace on Earth, good will to men" ring any bells? How about taking "Say hello to friends you know, and everyone you meet" to heart? I don't remember any carols about burying your neighbours up to their necks in snow."

"Sorry, Amanda," Belle said.

"I'm not the one you need to apologize too," Amanda told her.

Jack winced. Amanda had that mom voice down pat.

"Sorry, Jack. Please try to not throw snow into my yard," Belle said. Amanda nodded in satisfaction. He couldn't believe she bought it. Belle's smile obviously wasn't sincere; her dimple was nowhere in sight.

Sincere or not, now he had to be the bigger person too. It didn't matter that the whole thing had been an accident, and she had started it. "Sorry, Belle. I'll work on it."

"Very good. As you were before the snow fight," Amanda said before she grabbed her bags and shuffled down the street.

Belle wouldn't even look at him. She put her head down and went back to clearing the square in her yard. He'd managed to throw a lot of snow in there. He felt guilty until he was wracked with another shiver caused by the cold water pooling in his lower back. Jack slammed his shovel into a drift at the front door and stomped into his house. He'd made some progress today. He could do the rest next week. There was lots of time to leave Belle in the dust.

5. BELLE

The North Pole Unlimited cafeteria was huge. It had to be, since the company's December location was home to the head office and over a dozen departments. As Belle walked by the gigantic bulletin board at the cafeteria's entrance, she took a moment to mentally applaud the building's designer who had the forethought to know it would also be used as a meeting place and had placed a small stage along one wall to address an audience.

Today, the square platform was dominated by a large table and two fabric-covered boxes, and two women dressed in matching elf hats. As usual, Jilly Lewis-Fredericks was in the middle of the Christmas chaos. However, her normal sidekick, a very pregnant Joy Harkness, sat in the front row with her feet on a chair, relaxing while everybody around her kept an eye on her, hoping it wasn't the day she decided to go into labour.

Joy's replacement was Ginger Cardinal, another company elf with a romantic reputation. Belle was in awe that the company stayed running in December with all the matchmaking schemes the three women hatched. She was constantly signing "Congratulations" cards for various weddings where the bride and groom thanked at least one of them for getting them together.

"Okay, everybody, your attention, please," Jilly called from the stage. After the noise level dropped by half, she continued. "We are gathered here today for this year's Secret Santa gift exchange draw. The rules are as follows. Number one – you are only allowed to redraw if..."

"You draw your own name," the assembled crowd shouted back.

"That's right. If you draw your partner, you still have to be their Secret Santa at work," Jilly said. "Number two. Price limits are twenty dollars for..."

"Managers," people shouted.

"And ten for everybody else. This is a fun acknowledgement of the holidays, not a competition. We encourage cards, jokes, and handmade items. Last year I received a wonderful card from the president of Mars wishing me a merry Christmas and telling me I was out of this world. Which, of course, everybody already knows, but it was nice to see it in writing," Ginger joked. "Have fun with it."

"And three," Jilly added, much to Ginger's shock according to the look on her face, "all Totally Iced presents are subject to an HR tax."

Ginger bolted to her partner and mimed holding a hand over Jilly's mouth. "There is no three!" she announced with a laugh. "But it is time to get started. Please step forward when your name is called."

The women were fast and experienced with the system. Ginger called the names. Jilly reached into a gift bag and withdrew a piece of paper that had been folded in half and stapled. Belle waited her turn. She returned to her table and, with a quick check over her shoulder, looked at her name.

Her chin hit her chest in defeat. Of the hundreds of people who worked for North Pole Unlimited, why did she have to get Jack Foster?

She decided she wasn't getting the proper amount of sympathy when she shared the news with Carolyn at knit night.

"Your hat is looking great! You're almost ready to start the stripe. You could give it to your Secret Santa match, if it's a man. If the person has blue eyes, it'll really make them pop," her friend suggested.

"I am not giving it to—" Belle paused, looking around suspiciously. Not seeing anyone else from work, she whispered, "—Jack Foster." Even if he did have amazing blue eyes that the hat would match perfectly.

"You got my boss?" Carolyn whispered back.

"I know, right? Belle the Disaster Magnet strikes again. The only thing I want to give Mr. Perfect Christmas himself is a lump of coal and a wedgie."

Carolyn giggle-snorted. "Is this about the zip-ties?"

Belle stabbed the next stitch particularly fiercely with her knitting needle. "Maybe. Now I have to be nice to him."

"You'll live, Belle. It's not like you have to wine and dine him every day."

"You work with him. What would you give Mr. Christmas Award Shelf if you were his Secret Santa?"

Carolyn opened and closed her mouth a couple times before saying, "He likes candy."

A particularly cruel thought crossed Belle's mind. One that she could put into action and still claim as keeping within the spirit of the rules. "Candy? I can work with that."

6. JACK

His first Secret Santa gift came through the interoffice mail. Jack tipped the envelope, and a candy cane as thick as his thumb spilled onto his desk. He assumed the bright green meant it was spearmint-flavoured rather than peppermint – an assumption that was brutally dispelled when he popped a piece into his mouth and immediately spat it out. Dill pickle. He hadn't even known such a monstrosity existed. But then he tried another sliver. It was surprisingly not bad once he knew what to expect.

He'd suffered the horrible luck of drawing Belle Silver as his giftee. He'd hung her first present from her car's side mirror in a gift bag: an individual packet of luxury hot chocolate. Mexican hot chocolate with chili powder. He'd heard rumours of the decadent coffee counter in her office although he'd never been invited to try it himself. Jack had sampled the spicy hot cocoa last year and dumped the cup after two sips, but someone with such a refined palate as Belle might enjoy it. At least that was what he would claim if asked about it.

But Belle was the least of his problems at the moment. It was time to start preparing his yard for the contest. A predicted snowstorm was already rolling in and had already deposited two inches of snow on the ground. Still, Jack gamely got out his extension ladder and got to work on his holiday display. He'd been planning it for months. First, he had taken precise note of his house's dimensions the previous summer with a laser measure, noting every window and door. Then he'd plugged the numbers into a computer program to generate a symmetrical pattern for the one- and two-foot wooden snowflakes that he'd built and wired in his garage that autumn. They were the perfect complement to the one-foot wire-framed snowflakes he'd created for the massive evergreen in his front yard. He had even planned the placement of coloured bulbs for maximum impact. His snowflake-themed exhibition was going to be stunning.

The ladder was set. The snowflakes were piled high. The extension cords were looped to be raised without snagging or knotting on themselves. And then *she* appeared.

For reasons unknown, his next-door neighbour was dragging boxes of Christmas lights through her front door and arranging them in the clearing in her yard. Belle didn't even have any trees on her property.

Then a kerfuffle erupted across the street, distracting him from his wondering. His neighbours, Mr. and Mrs. Dempsey were waging a pitched battle on their steps.

"Gordon Donald Dempsey, get your butt back

inside!" Jack had never heard Clara raise her voice when she was working in the family's grocery store before she retired, but she was making up for it now. "Doctor Iverson specifically put shovelling on the "don't you dare" list after your heart attack."

"This driveway isn't going to clear itself, Clara. And you can't do it because of your back," Gord hollered as he trundled toward the shed in his backyard where Jack knew he kept his snowblower.

Jack hadn't been home the day the ambulance had screeched to a stop in front of the Dempsey's house a few months ago, but he'd heard about it from everybody. Gord was a good neighbour: he always gave a greeting when they were outside, he was happy to lend a hand when Jack had a two-person job that wasn't too strenuous and, most importantly, he didn't let his dog poop in Jack's yard. It was time to be a good neighbour in return.

"Hey, Gord, want a hand?" he called.

"No," Gord said.

"Yes, he does, thank you, Jack." Clara answered. "Belle, tell Gord he's being ridiculous. You were the one who saw him fall. I don't want to go through that again."

Belle crossed the street with her red plastic shovel over her shoulder like some kind of snowy dwarf. "Gord, you know you aren't supposed to be shovelling. I thought you hired somebody to clear your driveway this winter. I'll do it."

"I did hire someone. They flaked. Until I find a new company, somebody's got to do it. I'm not going to ask you when you have your own driveway to shovel."

Jack winced. "I can help too. If you let me use your snowblower—" he paused and looked over his shoulder at

Belle, who nodded in silent agreement, "—I'll bet that we can get this done in half an hour."

Belle began shovelling immediately. Jack took longer to get started because Gord had to show him how to start the finicky snowblower. But as soon as Jack was moving, both Dempseys went back inside and began supervising from the living room window. Belle cleared the steps and sidewalk and then began cleaning the edges of the driveway after he blew out the rest of it. As good as his word, twenty-nine minutes later, they were sweaty, snow-covered, and done.

Clara appeared on the front steps after he put away the snowblower. "Come inside, you two. I have cocoa and cookies as a thank you."

"Thanks, but we can't—" Jack bit back a yelp when Belle's shovel hit him in the backside.

"We'd love to!" Belle shouted. She plastered a grin on her face and, through gritted teeth, whispered, "If you make me miss one of her cookies, I will ruin you."

"Thank you, Clara" he corrected.

The Dempseys were ready for Christmas. They had a fake tree in the corner, covered in coordinated silver and gold ornaments and matching stockings hanging from the mantle over their electric fireplace. Christmas cards hung from a string which ran from one side of the window to the other. And on the table was an old, two-tiered China tray filled with shortbread, peanut butter marshmallow squares, and toasty, honey-coloured squares that Clara called the Bee's Knees. Jake's mouth watered at the sight of it all.

"We were wondering when you two were going to join forces and do a double yard display," Clara said as she handed him a mug of steaming hot chocolate topped with mini marshmallows.

"Between the two of you, I'll bet you'd be able to stop traffic," Gord agreed.

"Never!" he blurted. Jack couldn't imagine anything he'd hate to do more.

"Oh, no," Belle said. "We couldn't. Ever. We have... completely different styles."

Jack jumped on the excuse, even if it meant agreeing with Belle. "Totally."

"Jack is a professional marketer specializing in Christmas. His yard could be an advertisement for Christmas lights."

He bit into a piece of Bee's Knees instead of biting his tongue over the insinuation that his yard was a sterile advertisement rather than a heartfelt holiday display. Clara and Gord beamed like Belle had delivered a great compliment. "Belle, on the other hand, goes for more relaxed, homemade vibes," he said.

Belle knew what he meant. "Thank you so much for the cookies, but I have to get back to work. My lights aren't going to hang themselves," she told the friendly couple.

"It's true," Jack agreed. "There's still an hour of daylight and I need every minute."

They made their goodbyes to the Dempseys, but he paused at the foot of their driveway. Belle looked at him expectantly. "The forecast is calling for twenty to thirty centimeters today and tonight. Which means we're going to get three to four times more than what we just cleared for them."

"Want to meet back here again after supper and give everything another pass? Seven o'clock?" she asked.

"Deal."

Belle took off in one direction, shovel over her shoulder. He headed the other way. As frustrating as dealing with Belle always was, he couldn't deny that she was a good neighbour. And she'd done him a huge favour.

Those Bee's Knees were out of this world.

7. BELLE

Belle had a strange hankering. The chili hot chocolate mix that she'd received from her Secret Santa had been an unusual flavour. When she'd tried it, she wasn't sure whether or not she liked it. But she hadn't been able to stop thinking about it. She needed to find another packet to decide. In the meantime, she'd have to make do with a peppermint mocha from the Pumpkin Patch after another evening of putting together her front yard display.

It had been a long couple of days. She'd spent most of them arguing with Jack Foster over emails about his marketing campaigns for the next year. He didn't grasp the concept of Christmastown...yet. It was her job to make sure he did. Belle understood North's instructions perfectly.

She had been hired by North's grandmother to help expand the company beyond its humble mail-order cata-logue-turned-online-store beginnings. North Pole Unlimited had thrilled customers for decades with its sentimental advertising and quality goods. Adelaide Klassen had wanted to start an in-house recording division before she retired. She brought in Belle to create a music and audio book recording facility and catalogue.

It had taken two years for Belle to get it up and running, but now it was a major arm of the company. Then North Santana, Adelaide's successor and granddaughter, had taken over the reins, with her brothers Noel and Nick running other departments. The siblings wanted to grow the company again, going in a new direction with the biggest special project yet.

Christmastown had been four years in the making so far. North had pulled Belle into the vision from the very beginning. Belle believed in the idea with all of her heart: the world needed a family-friendly, year round Christmas-themed park. No mice, no superheroes, just a red-suited man with a plan and a team of helpers backing him up. The plan was incredible, full of rides and activities, shops and restaurants, and stages for entertainment. Nobody could spend a day there and not come out filled with Christmas spirit.

Except maybe Jack Foster. He didn't get it. Belle was beginning to fear he never would.

She pushed him from her mind and was almost home free when she heard the gasp and the shout coming from the front lobby. Belle saw Joy Harkness sitting on a desk chair in the middle of the corridor. Barb, the normally cheery receptionist, hovered over her. Both women were in their coats and toques.

"What's wrong?" Belle asked.

"Nothing, I'm fine," Joy said first. The red-haired woman put her hand on her abdomen and winced.

"You are not fine," Barb tattled. "Decker left to get his truck, but he's parked in the far lot. Joy was standing here waiting, but then she got light-headed and almost fainted."

"I did not almost faint. I don't have time. I have too much to do. We have to finish packing. We're supposed to be out of the apartment by December fifteenth. Then once we're in the new house, we have to decorate it. I'd skip this year, but Charlie is terrified that Santa won't find us if the house isn't done. I don't have time for a tantrum from Joy Junior and she isn't even born yet!"

"Take a breath, Joy. I'll see if Decker's here," Belle offered. She stepped through the glass double doors and was hit in the face by a gust of arctic wind. As she blinked the snow crystals out of her eyes, she could see a SUV pulling up. Then she realized it was Jack Foster, not Decker. Instead of heading to an open space in the second row, Jack stopped in front of the entrance, flicked on his emergency lights, and got out of the vehicle.

"You can't park here."

"Give it a rest, Parking Patrol. I'm only running in for five minutes."

Of all the self-absorbed, dismissive jerks! "Not for me, Foster. Decker's gone to get his truck from the far lot because Joy's sick in the lobby." She saw a similar white vehicle pull around the corner. "Here he is."

Jack tossed his keychain to her. "Will you move my car while I help Decker with Joy?"

"Of course." His SUV smelled like evergreens thanks to the cardboard tree hanging from the rearview mirror. Belle carefully drove to the end of the lot, then pulled into the second row of parking. She wasn't used to driving anything as big as his SUV, so it took her two tries to park squarely between the lines. She even chose a spot close to the doors.

By the time Belle returned to the lobby, Barb was holding the door open, Jack had his arm around Joy's waist, and Decker was adjusting the car seat. Joy was still talking about packing.

"How about you give me your keys, and I'll take a load of boxes over while you and Decker are at the doctor?" Belle heard Jack ask.

"If you're sure, that would be great," Decker said. The tall, blond man handed Jack a key ring. "Don't worry, we don't have a security system. Any full boxes you can move would be great. They'll all labelled because somebody is a list freak."

"My lists are saving your butt now, aren't they?" Joy muttered as she smacked Decker's hand away from her seatbelt. He backed away and bumped into Jack.

"I'll handle everything," Jack promised.

"Thank you," the couple chorused.

Decker's bump knocked Jack's hat to the ground. Then the panicky papa stepped on it in the shuffle as the men tried to close Joy's door. Once she was safely buckled and Decker was pulling away, Jack recovered his mud-caked toque, and they reconvened in the lobby.

Belle handed Jack his keys. "You're in row two."

"I saw. Thanks."

Barb sniffed. "Do you think she's going to be okay? Joy's so sweet. She's my number one cat-sitter when I go on vacation."

"I think she'll be fine. Decker was taking her to a doctor's appointment anyway, so she'll be examined right away," Belle said, remembering their conversation at lunch.

"That's good to know," Jack agreed. He twisted his dirty toque in his hand.

"Listen, this was pretty stressful. Do you want to come back to my office for a cup of tea or cocoa or something before you drive home?" Belle turned to look at her nemesis, to make sure he knew that he was included after being so helpful. "I'll make the good stuff," she promised.

Jack's blue eyes blinked at her. "No. But thank you. I'm only here for a minute. I have to get going. And now I've promised to move boxes. Listen, if you hear anything, would you..."

"Of course," Belle agreed. Work conflicts were one thing, but folks in December stepped up for their neighbours. When Jack left, she felt for a split second like she'd missed an opportunity.

"I heard Noel from IT talking about your vanilla lattes," Barb said. Then she hiccupped and brushed a tear off her cheek. "They sound pretty good."

"This definitely merits a vanilla latte. Come on. I'll ply you with coffee and get you to spill all your outdoor lighting secrets when it comes to the December Light Spectacular since you were a runner-up last year."

"Well, first of all, we have tons of zip-ties to secure all our string lights," Barb began.

"Seriously? Does everybody know about the zip-ties?" Belle asked.

"Yep."

"That's just great."

8. JACK

"Great news!" North announced over the video screen. "Joy had an inspired thought about how to get you excited about Christmastown."

Half of that statement was good news. "Joy's back? How is she doing?" Jack asked.

"She's fine. She will be cutting back on her hours but she's doing great. It doesn't matter. Decker is keeping her hospital go-bag within reach at all times. He showed me the baby hat that Belle made that Joy is insisting they bring, along with a two-pound bag of jerky and Joy's father's Rubic's Cube."

Jack's brain stuttered over the list of items. "That last one sounds like a painful projectile if her labour is difficult."

"Are you going to say no to a pregnant woman?"

"Absolutely not!"

"Smart man. Anyway, Joy had a great idea, which is the reason you and Belle are going on a field trip."

"What? Where? When? Most importantly, why with Belle?" Jack and his team had been brainstorming about Christmastown for days with no results. He never would have guessed that an amusement park full of rides, activities and food centred around one of the most celebrated events of the year would be the project that broke him. Yet, here he was, trying to come up with an idea that was better than a picture of a kid in a toque with his finger up his nose.

"Meet me in Belle's office after lunch. Bring your coat. If you don't have proper outdoor gear, swing by maintenance and they'll set you up."

Jack was willing to try anything at this point. Even working with Belle. "I'll be there."

He'd been in the Special Projects reception area before, but not during the holiday season. Jack nodded approvingly to himself at the decorations. No wonder Belle recognized the quality of the Christmas layouts he'd produced for the company. Her office was worthy of any catalogue shoot. The only things out of place were files and boxes and things in active use, which raised her in his estimation because she'd planned around work, rather than leaving her staff to work around the décor. He wouldn't have gone with a silver and lilac theme, but colour was a personal choice.

"Oh good, you're here." North entered like a whirlwind, with a phone in one hand and a tablet in the other. A charging cable trailed from her suit jacket pocket.

"What's the plan?" Jack asked.

"Come into Belle's office and we'll discuss it."

Jack blinked twice when he got a good look around

Belle's private sanctum. It was nothing like the public area. In fact, three of the four walls were completely barren of Christmas décor altogether. The fourth wall, however, looked like an elf had exploded on the premises.

An ugly green ball of garland took up a large portion of the counter beside the coffee maker. A string of old, multi-hued mini lights was haphazardly pinned above it all. It resembled a basement bar from the 1980s. The section of wall that ran from Belle's coffee counter to her office door was the most colourful he'd ever seen. Art covered nearly every square inch. Talent levels ranged from finger-paintings signed with tiny handprints, to crayon drawings on copy paper, to paintings on canvas that were as good as fine arts student projects.

"I see you've found Belle's Silver Gallery. She brings in her family's art rather than choosing from the corporate catalogue," North explained.

Jack could see that Belle had embraced the entire chaotic spread and had hung them all with love. "It's a lot." He wasn't criticizing. Just commenting.

"Belle says her artistic soul runs more to exploded unicorn than pastel watercolours."

"I can see that."

"I have nine nieces and nephews," Belle bragged from behind her desk. "I get their masterpieces on a regular basis. Plus, we do family art nights. I buy shadow box frames in bulk to store it all. Corporate can't compete."

Jack thought of the nursery school turkey his younger nephew had sent him in October for Thanksgiving. He had no memory of what he'd done with it after video-calling his sister and telling her that he got it. It definitely hadn't made it onto his refrigerator.

North called them to order by sitting in one of Belle's

guest chairs. "I have two other meetings this afternoon so let's get down to it. Joy said something to me yesterday that got me thinking. Jack, we've shown you the plans and maps and blueprints, but you haven't seen Christmastown with your own eyes. You need to know what you're selling. Joy suggested that you visit the property so you can experience it in real life instead of on paper. Aside from me, the person who knows Christmastown best is Belle. I'm too busy to go, so I'm sending the two of you to the site so you can see the scale of what we're aiming to achieve."

"That's not necessary." It was an unnecessary punishment. There was nothing Belle could show him that would help. In fact, being forced to spend the afternoon with her might actually extinguish any lingering sparks of creativity he had.

"Is that why you asked me to go to the site today?" Belle exclaimed. "I thought I was checking to see if traffic to the North Pole Evergreens lot was interfering with construction and blocking the road."

"That too. We're creating a new entrance to the tree farm in the spring, but right now, all the customers and construction crews are using the same turn-off. Take Jack and show him Christmastown. Make him see, Belle. Make him believe it," North ordered.

Belle looked as thrilled as he was about their new afternoon plans. But she worked for North, just like he did. She gave him an awful smile, then said, "Grab your coat and let's go. We'll take my car. I have to stop at my place. I had a meeting in Animal Care and one of the dogs had an accident."

"No problem." He didn't even make a joke. He'd had meetings in Animal Care too.

"You can come in if you want," Belle said as they

pulled into her driveway. "It'll be warmer than waiting in the car while I change."

He'd never been inside her home before. He'd only caught glimpses through the window.

It looked like...

It was beyond anything...

If Santa in his formal red suit and the Grinch in all his greenness had been wrestling in Belle's living room, this would be the result. He'd never seen so much eclectic décor in such a small place. Unlike her office, there was no theme. Antique European St. Nicholas carvings sat next to fat snowmen with top hats. Holiday candles fought with snow globes for shelf space on a fake fireplace mantle. Every piece of furniture was covered with a blanket displaying a different holiday scene. Not only did he have to close his eyes before the discord made his stomach turn over, but his brain rebelled at the differences between Belle's office and her home.

"I'm ready."

"Your house is very different than your reception area," he said.

"I hired a professional to do the public facing areas at work. They had to meet corporate standards. My house is just me."

"I can see that." He needed to investigate her decorator's portfolio. If she started with a base that Belle gave her, she was a miracle worker. "Is that painting an earlier work of the niece or nephew who did the snowy cabin scene in your office? That one was really good. This one is a little less refined."

"No, this one is mine," Belle said shortly. "Come on. Let's go."

"Yes, please." He hadn't meant to make her feel bad

about the painting. But he hadn't been wrong either. The one in her office had been much better than hers.

Their destination was about fifteen minutes away. The highway turnoff was marked with a big wooden sign announcing that they'd arrived at North Pole Evergreens. Belle drove carefully on the ice and ruts, then turned south when the road split.

"Both the tree lot and Christmastown are getting new signs. The gates will be locked when they are closed to prevent people from abusing the parking lots," Belle said as they got out of her car. "Right now, this lot is being used for staging."

He could see that. A trailer full of lumber sat at one end, between a bulldozer and an excavator.

"We'll check in at the construction trailer, and then I'll give you the tour."

The area was massive: at least the size of a city block. Snow drifts leaned against concrete foundations. House-wrap covered several buildings that were waiting for their exteriors to be finished.

"Just inside the gates, we're going to have the main customer services building. On the other side of the entrance will be the nine-hole mini-golf course," Belle said as she led him around. She pointed out future stores, restaurants, and the site for the splash pad and skating rink. She explained that there were three lots designated for carnival rides which were arriving in the spring. Belle showed him the route that would take visitors through various Christmas vignettes—the same forest path that the hayrides and sleigh rides would take around the park. "Plus, we'll have "elfie" stations throughout the park for fun photos."

"Are you going to have bonfire pits in the winter?

Because this is ridiculous." He slapped his hands together, desperate to get the blood flowing to his extremities.

"You should have worn real mitts."

"These are real mittens."

Belle scoffed. "Those are Toronto mittens. Get yourself some fleece-lined leather ones before your fingers fall off, Foster."

"Is the tour done yet?"

"Almost." She dragged him to the exact centre of the empty space. She spread her arms wide and announced, "This is the bandstand. Christmas carol sing-a-longs, bands and other performers, and Santa reading "A Visit from St. Nicholas" to shut down the park every day," Belle concluded.

Jack had stopped talking halfway through his tour. He wasn't annoyed with Belle's chipper explanations, or the fact that he was nearly frozen. He was annoyed with himself. "This is a theme park," he said.

"Yes."

"A theme park," he repeated.

"That is what North and I have been telling you. For months."

"You said it was a theme park, but I thought you meant an amusement park. I thought it was going to be all carnival rides and food trucks."

"We will have those things," Belle insisted.

"Yes, but this is so much more. It's like a fully functional Santa's Village, or..."

"A *town*? Full of *Christmas*?" She sounded the words out slowly.

"Okay, I am an idiot." Jack laughed at himself. "I don't hear you arguing with me."

"It's too cold to argue." Belle pointed at her car and

began walking toward it. "Do you understand the vision now?"

No wonder North had shot down every idea he'd had. His team had been concentrating on the commerciality of Christmastown. He was so focused on what he could sell to the family member purchasing the admission tickets that he'd skipped over the families themselves. "I think that I'm finally starting to."

"Great. Terrific. Let's get out of this wind."

Jack didn't think she was being short with him. The sun was going down and the wind was picking up. He was freezing. "Good idea. I have to get home and package my mother's chocolate covered shortbread cookies for the bake sale this weekend. What are you donating?"

"My time. Helen Gauthier asked me to step in as treasurer and cash table coordinator instead of donating baked goods this year." She smiled, but he noticed a sheen in her eyes. Before he could comment, she dabbed it away with her mitten. "Wow, that's a powerful wind. Anyway, I think I'm going to claim executive privilege and buy a couple trays before we open. Otherwise, there won't be anything left."

As a joke, Jack was going to ask why she wouldn't donate a tray of something anyway. But her unshed tears gave him pause. Belle had taken a lot of ribbing over her contribution's return last year. Bringing it up again at this point might be a step to far. They might be in competition, and all was fair in love and war, but he didn't want to be a jerk about it.

"Let's get out of here," he said instead.

INTERLUDE

Interlude

Friday, December 9

"How did it go?" Jilly Lewis-Fredericks asked. She was supposed to be in the Human Resources offices preparing a report for her boss, Nick Klassen. Instead, she was in the Animal Care department with Joy and Ginger, surrounded by crates of dog and cat toys. It wasn't her usual haunt, but her current project took priority over her work. Nick would understand.

"North took the bait. She is sending Belle and Jack to Christmastown today so he can get a feel for the place," Joy Harkness reported.

"Well done!" Jilly reached into the bag she was carrying and pulled out a box of assorted Christmas cookies. She pushed it toward Joy, who waved them away.

"I'm off cookies until after the baby is born. She has decided that chocolate gives her heartburn," Joy said.

"All cookies?" Ginger asked, horrified. "Not even

shortbread? That's the most inoffensive cookie in the world."

"Dill. She wants dill-flavoured everything," Joy groused. "I am not amused." She shifted in her seat, but Jilly could see she still wasn't comfortable.

"My sympathies." Jilly still remembered her pregnancy cravings with her son Dan twenty-five years later. "Were there any problems in seeding the idea with North?"

"Of course not." Joy yawned. "Nobody ever suspects the pregnant lady."

"That's why we had you do it," Ginger said.

Jilly grinned. Her protégés had learned well. "There is a slight chance that Belle and Jack will kill each other," she noted. She twisted her wedding ring around her fourth finger. "The December Light Spectacular is going to be a bloodbath unless we get them on the same page before Judging Day."

"Do you think that they'd sabotage each other?" Ginger asked in alarm.

"I think that if someone says the words "zip-tie" to Belle one more time, she's going to snap and buy a space heater to melt every snowflake on Jack's property, so he has nothing to decorate."

"That's extreme. Maybe they'll burn off some of that animosity with their Secret Santa gifts. They wouldn't welch on them, would they?" Joy asked.

Jilly laughed. "No. They both fear me too much."

"You say that like it's a good thing," Joy noted.

"Let's be honest. It's best for everyone if they do. They'll thank me later. Adelaide and I did great with you and Decker, didn't we?"

Joy patted her belly. "You did okay." She stopped

squirming and struggled to her feet. "I need to go to the bathroom. Again. Let me know if Jack and Belle's field trip goes well, okay?"

Jilly gently grabbed Joy's arm and helped her find her balance. "I'm assuming that it'll go swimmingly. I'm banking on the spirit of the season."

"And if it doesn't?"

Jilly flinched. "If it doesn't, I think the whole town is going to know."

9. JACK

Jack parked beside a classic 1940s red pick-up. Traffic into and out of the parking lot was a constant flow of locals wanting to shop at the December Extravaganza Craft and Bake Show, one of the biggest events in the town's calendar. He had dropped off his mother's chocolate covered shortbread the night before. At the same time, he'd made a mental list of things to buy when he returned the next day.

He considered activating the chemical mitten warmers that his Secret Santa had given him, but he didn't want to waste them on the short walk from his car to the community centre. He'd save them for when he really needed them. Like the next time he had to go on a field trip with Belle.

As Jack paid his entry fee and began inspecting the folding tables laden with goodies, he wished he had eaten lunch before he came. He was going to need a box to tote his haul to his car. He was already juggling half a dozen butter tarts, a tray of Nanaimo squares, and a slab of vinarterta. He wasn't done, though—he was still on the hunt for some of Clara Dempsey's Bee's Knees Squares.

He stopped to watch the six pre-teens hard at work on the gingerbread house challenge. Each one had six pieces of gingerbread to turn into a house, four gingerbread people, and full access to the icing and decorations table. Five of the contestants had upright buildings. Some were attaching candies to rooftops. Others were fashioning Christmas trees from green gumdrops and toothpicks. A red-faced boy at the end of the row stared at his collapsed house walls with a look of defeat that turned to absolute panic when one of the judges announced they had seven minutes left. The boy's father stepped out of the crowd and crouched to talk to his son.

"That's Chace." The last time Jack had seen Belle, she'd been at the cash table. He hadn't noticed her sneak up beside him. "Excuse me," she said as she squeezed by.

"Was that Belle Silver?" Chad Parker from his office asked. "She didn't bake the gingerbread the kids are using for construction, did she? No wonder they're having problems." Chad laughed like it was the best joke ever.

Jack had heard the story. The whole company had. But this laughter was a little too loud for an event that had happened a year ago. "I don't think so. Are you still talking about her gumdrop cake?"

"That. The gingerbread the year before. The fudge the year before that. Usually people are warned when they are buying Belle's donations, but nobody's said anything this year."

Jack stopped paying attention when he saw Belle approach the young food architect. She reached into her purse and pulled out a plastic bag with something yellow inside. He was too far away to see exactly what it was. She handed it to Chace's dad, then spoke earnestly to Chace. The boy sat a little straighter, then nodded. Belle returned to her spot in the crowd. Chace's father said something, and Chace started to smile before he raced around the table and began working on his gingerbread house again. Chace's dad reappeared two minutes later and handed off a package.

Five minutes later, the judges rang a bell, and the six contestants stood proudly behind their houses.

Jack applauded with the rest of the crowd, but he clapped especially hard for Chace's scene. Rather than try to fix his house, the kid had added plastic construction hats to his gingerbread people, turning them into a construction crew. A toy bulldozer sat on the board, its blade in the house's living room.

He laughed out loud when Chace announced the name of his house. While the other kids had "Candy Cane Cottage" and "Cookie Cabin", Chace said, "Decoration Demolition Day."

Jack wasn't surprised that Chace didn't win. But he did get words of encouragement from the judges who congratulated him for not giving up and for pivoting to a new idea when his first didn't work.

"You gave him the construction hats," Jack said quietly to Belle.

"I did."

"You just happened to have them in your purse?"

"No, I brought them on purpose. Every year or two, there is a kid who crashes and burns in this contest. I figured this year, I could potentially save somebody from public humiliation."

"It's all in good humour," Jack protested.

"Not when a middle-schooler is the one being laughed at. Look, I know that I'm the town joke. I had to hire somebody to decorate my office because my sense of style is so bad. They wouldn't let me donate anything because I can't bake. I can deal with it. I'm an adult. A kid shouldn't have to," Belle said.

"That's not true. We laugh with you, not at you, when you have a mishap. It's not your fault that you're not very good at Christmas," he said.

He thought he was being diplomatic. Belle didn't take it that way. She leaned closer and gave him a fearsome smile, no dimple in sight. "Jack Foster, I will have you know that I am excellent at Christmas. I'm just not good at being perfect. It's too bad that some people can't tell the difference."

As she stormed back to the cash desk, Jack laughed it off. She obviously thought she'd insulted him, but she'd missed her shot: how could her considering him being perfect be anything but a compliment?

10. BELLE

Whoever was sprinkling Christmas magic all over December evidently missed her house, Bell thought grumpily. She'd woken up to a dumping of snow, heavy enough that she'd had to clear her sidewalk and driveway. She shovelled first, then went inside for a shower, but even rushing meant she was ten minutes later than she wanted to be. The delay had given Jack enough time to get to work first and take the corner parking spot.

After that, she had to wait in the lobby as a mob slowly made its way down the main corridor. "What's going on?" Belle asked Barb.

"It's Joy."

That didn't sound good. "Is she okay?"

"She's having contractions."

Belle knew that to Decker and Joy's delight, they were due to have a Christmas baby. But this was much too early. "Where's Decker?"

"Getting the truck from the far lot. Again."

"Who do I have to talk to in order to have pregnancy parking assigned in the first row?"

Barb grimaced. "That would be Nick. Jilly already asked after the last time. He put her off because they were negotiating with the transportation division for their next contract. Trust me, he's going to be hearing about it as soon as he arrives today. Jilly already asked me to have the head of the maintenance department report directly to Human Resources when he gets in."

"As long as somebody is on it," Belle said.

With one arm gripping Nick Klassen and the other holding onto Noel Sprouse, Joy arrived in the lobby a couple of minutes later. She'd paused halfway down the corridor for a full minute, doubled over. Nick and Noel's faces turned white, but they hadn't said a word. Joy's red faced focused on her. She stared Belle straight in the eye and said, "Shoot."

"What? What's wrong?"

"I don't know if Decker remembered to pack your awesome baby hat shower present in my hospital bag," Joy said.

"We'll make sure you get it in time if I have to break into your place myself," Belle promised. Then Decker pulled to the curb, and everybody in the lobby tried to lift the protesting redhead into the front seat.

Belle waved as they drove away. A small smile escaped her lips even in the serious situation. Joy liked her baby hat so much that she wanted the baby to wear it home! It seemed like Carolyn was right, and her knitting was finally at a gift giving level. Maybe she wouldn't embarrass herself anonymously when she gave Jack his next Secret Santa present.

The next night, Belle was wishing she could keep the wool hat for herself. A mid-December Arctic Vortex meant the entire province was suffering under a front of extra cold arctic air. Unfortunately, her decorations couldn't wait for Mother Nature to get over her tantrum, so Belle was outside and up to her freezing nose in tools.

Her decorating theme this year was "Rocking Around the Christmas Tree." Her problem was that she did not have an evergreen in her front yard. Belle could have used a simple artificial tree, but that wouldn't be impressive enough to win over any judges. Instead, she had used her hard-won zip-ties to attach strings of Christmas lights to hula hoops of various sizes. If her contraption worked as it was supposed to, as she raised her main line on the flagpole, it would lift the consecutive rings and produce a twenty-foot tree made entirely of lights.

In theory.

Reality was a Grinch. The plastic zip-ties kept cracking and breaking in the cold whenever the wind shook the strings, causing them to tangle or hang limply against the pole. Belle wanted to cry in frustration, but she knew her tears would only freeze on her cheeks. She needed this to work. The zip-ties were the most practical connectors she'd come up with.

She hadn't even tried to raise the speaker yet.

"Howdy, neighbour!"

The shout came from the other side of her property line. It was immediately followed by the loud ratcheting and rattling of an extension ladder being hoisted to its full length.

Jack Foster held the base of the ladder as he slowly tipped it against the front of his house. "What a beautiful day to hang some lights, huh?"

He climbed the ladder like he was part mountain goat, carrying a wooden snowflake the size of his arm. He magically attached it to the side of his house, zipped back to the ground, grabbed another, and was up the ladder again before she could blink. He reached for the cord dangling from the first snowflake and plugged it into the base of the second. They both sprang to life.

It looked...good. His house was going to look like it was hand-painted by Jack Frost himself. Belle scowled. Jack probably chose the idea just to make the play on his own name. At least his ears looked cold in his ratty hat. Whether he knew it or not, he was going to owe her one. It was a small comfort, but it counted.

"Why aren't your zip-ties breaking in this cold like mine are, Foster?" she called.

He looked down from his ladder. "I used them to hold the lights to the snowflake frames. The frames move but the lights don't. As long as I don't bump them around, they'll hold. Having problems?"

"I wouldn't say that." Belle would never admit defeat. She was like Einstein; she was finding new ways not to do things.

"Are you going to give me any hints as to what you're planning?"

"You first, neighbour."

"I think surprises will be good for both of us," Jack said.

"I'm going inside. Good night." Belle left the tangle of lights and hoops in her yard. She needed to thaw her hands around a mug of hot chocolate and research fasteners that were good to forty below. If she was really lucky, she'd find something before she headed into the city the next day. She could pick up her solution on her way to Knit Night.

Belle carefully threaded a safety line through all the stitches on her cable needle. She was casting off Jack's hat. She wasn't about to lose all her work when she could take precautions to prevent it. If she was making a spite hat, she was making it to the best of her limited ability.

"Did you hear anything about Joy?" she asked her friend.

"She's still in the hospital," Carolyn reported. "Ginger Malone visited her today. Joy is super worried about getting everything moved into their new house. Ginger's organizing a volunteer moving crew."

"I can help!"

"Too late. It filled up immediately. They are working tonight and tomorrow. Ginger even arranged for a cleaning crew for the apartment. They'll be all moved in by the end of the week."

"That's good." Belle went silent as she concentrated on slipping the needle through the last of her stitches. She pulled the yarn tight, and the hole at the top of the hat disappeared. She was finally done. She quickly tied off the yarn, weaved in the tail, and dropped the completed hat on the table in front of her.

"Belle, that's incredible!" Carolyn exclaimed. "Look! You nailed the colour change of the stripe both times."

"It's not perfect," Belle said. She choked on the word. She hadn't told Carolyn about her conversation with Jack at the bake sale. Or his assessment of her holiday skills. "I didn't drop any stitches, but the tension is uneven. Plus, my cast off stitches are lopsided."

"Your tension will even out with practice. You did it, Belle. Be proud of yourself."

"Is it good enough for your boss?" Belle asked. That was the real test. She'd been knitting extra fast ever since Jack's toque had been trampled. But she didn't want to give him this one if it wasn't up to a decent standard.

"Absolutely," her bestie swore. "It will keep his head warm, and he'll look good wearing it. By the way, this is a friendly reminder that my birthday is at the end of January and I look fantastic in pink."

"You're silly."

"I'm serious. When is Secret Santa going to give this amazing present to their person?"

"Secret Santa will put it in tomorrow's interoffice mail."

"Cool! Maybe I'll be there when he opens it. I'll let you know how it goes."

"Terrific."

Carolyn handed the hat back and recovered her sock needles. "Did you get anything else from your Secret Santa so far? I got a Cadbury Fruit and Nut chocolate bar. From England, so it's the good chocolate."

"Lucky you. I got a keychain." Belle was disappointed, actually. The keychain had a plastic "B" on a ring, and a carabiner clip for attaching it to her car fob. She didn't expect anything expensive, but she had hoped whoever had drawn her name would have personalized her gift a little more.

Carolyn patted her on the head. "I'll share my chocolate bar with you."

"Just like the old days," Belle said with a laugh. "No, it's okay. You enjoy it. I know it's your favourite. I'll cross my fingers that my Secret Santa finishes his deliveries with a bang."

11. JACK

His trip to Christmastown was paying off. Now that Jack knew he could plan for more than just amusement park rides, ideas were flying thick and fast across the conference room table as his team brainstormed.

The meeting broke when they saw the mail clerk pushing a cart down the hall. "Secret Santa deliveries!" Chad called.

"Fine, take ten minutes to refill your coffee cups, but I want you back here ready to keep going," Jack yelled at their backs as they all took off.

He'd sent his second gift to Belle two days earlier. While making her drive to Winnipeg for supplies for her yard display was fair game, he wanted to beat Belle on the finished product, not because she couldn't put her plan into action. He'd been as surprised as she was that the cold weather caused the zip-ties to break. He'd been thinking about it, and he figured that metal carabiners would work better in the weather. He'd sent her one on a keychain as a hint. The rest was up to her.

"Hey, Jack, Secret Santa delivered something to you too," Carolyn said as she returned with a bulky envelope.

His other team members retook their seats as well, chatting as they compared chocolate bars and gift cards to Norma's Buns in town.

Jack carefully slit the sealed package and poured the contents onto the conference room table. At first the soft, squishy green and blue lump was unrecognizable. Then he picked it up, stuck his hand into the open end and realized what he was holding.

"Wow, that's some hat, Jack," Scott Holmes, his graphic designer, commented.

Scott was being kind. The colours matched well. That was all he could say in the toque's favour. The edge of the ribbed brim was uneven, and the hat puckered on one side where a cluster of stitches were noticeably smaller than the rest. Jack pulled it onto his head, then posed like a model. "It screams Christmas, doesn't it?"

"It screams something," Chad said.

"Help?" Scott added.

Jack snickered. But he cut off abruptly when Carolyn pushed herself away from the table. "You are not knit-worthy, Jack," she announced.

"What?" he asked.

"Knit-worthy. Worthy of having somebody knit something for you," she explained slowly.

"We're just teasing," Jack protested. It's not as if his new hat could be mistaken for anything commercially made. It was obviously an amateur attempt.

Carolyn was not appeased. Her brown eyes sparked

when she said, "There isn't a single store in December that sells yarn. Did you know that?"

He didn't have a chance to answer because Carolyn barreled on. "She-ecret Santa," she stuttered, "either had to go into the city to buy that yarn or order it online. They picked a pattern and chose the colours to make it work. They ordered the yarn, paid for it, and brought it home. Then they spent hours hand-knitting it. And then, they decided that you were a worthy recipient of all that time and effort and creativity. If you don't like it, you don't have to wear it, but the very least you can do when you get a gift you don't like is say thank-you and set it aside without mocking it," Carolyn said stiffly. "Excuse me, I need more coffee if this is the start to my day."

Scott and Chad fell silent, but that was nothing compared to the stillness that fell over Jack. His department had paid hundreds of dollars for handmade hats and scarves for various photo shoots because the accessories could be made to order. The quality of those bespoke items was second-to-none. But he'd never considered what it took to get that final product, namely, all the less-than-perfect versions that came before it. All those artisans had started with something like the toque that was on his head. And while those were for profit, the one he was wearing was made with nothing but good intentions and love for the craft.

Jack pulled it off and set it carefully in the centre of the conference table. He'd been told. If he gave it the smallest bit of reflection, he had it coming. He'd violated the entire spirit of Secret Santa: first by using it to fuel his Christmas decoration fight with Belle, then by claiming an obviously home-made gift was not up to his standards.

Before he could apologize and correct himself to his

team, Carolyn popped her head into the conference room. Her glare had been replaced with one of concern. "Jack, there's an urgent family call on hold in your office."

He sprinted down the hall. "Hello?"

The reply was a sniffle. "Uncle Jack? You have to help me!"

"What's wrong, Joey? Is anybody hurt?" Joey should have contacted one of his parents if that were the case, or his grandparents if both had been injured. Jack lived out of province and was far down the emergency call list.

"I ruined Christmas!"

Ah, it was that kind of emergency. Still traumatic for a primary schooler, but no blood involved. "What happened?" he asked.

"I tried to wrap Mom's present. I ripped the last of the Christmas paper."

"Your dad will buy more paper for you, kiddo. Why don't you ask him for help?"

"No, this is my present to Mom. I have to do it myself. I tried to do it like you wrapped Grandma's present last year. That was so cool! All I'm doing is making a mess."

"I'm an adult and I had to take two classes to learn how to wrap gifts like that. You're only eleven. No wonder you're having problems, Joey."

"You really had to take lessons on how to wrap presents?" his nephew asked suspiciously.

"Kiddo, I hired an expert wrapper to teach me. Can you hang up and vid-chat me on your phone so I can see what you've done?" Jack asked. He really needed to get back to his meeting, but at least this was one problem that might have an easy fix.

Then seconds later, he was looking at two shoebox corners poking through green and silver striped paper.

"Yeah, the corners are really tough with that technique. You did really well getting so far on your own," Jack commiserated.

"How did you do it?"

"I had four rolls of paper and two practice boxes. I can send you the link to a demonstration video if you want to go that hard. Or I can tell you the secret I used to fix my mistakes on Grandma's present," he offered.

"What secret?"

"The tissue paper roses in the corners were there to cover the tape."

"No way!"

"Those corners were murder!" Jack still hadn't perfected them. "Do you have any tissue paper? Your mom probably has some for using with gift bags."

"Yes, she has some."

"Here's what you're going to do. You are going to cut a bunch of small paper snowflakes and layer them across the corners. Two or three thick. That way it'll look deliberate. Be careful when you tape them. They'll tear easily."

Joey lay a sheet of white tissue paper over his box. "That'll look pretty good! Thanks, Uncle Jack."

"Any time, kiddo. What else have you been up to?"

"Grandma and I made her chocolate dipped short-bread this weekend."

"What? She taught you the super secret family recipe? That's incredible!"

"What recipe? It's Walker shortbread fingers dipped in melted chocolate chips."

Jack's ears began to ring. "Excuse me? What?" His mother's renowned, even fought-over, Christmas delicacies were storebought cookies dipped in chocolate chips?

"Right?" his nephew laughed. "I always thought she

spent hours slaving over the oven. Nope. You melt the chocolate in the microwave and dunk the cookie. It was super easy. Dad couldn't tell the ones I made from the ones she made. They all think I'm a genius now. Grandma says I'm her baking heir and that I'm going to take over her empire."

"Fantastic, Joey. Look, I have to get back to work. Let me know how the snowflakes work, okay?"

"Sure. Thanks, Uncle Jack."

Jack lay his cell phone face down on his desk. Then promptly dropped his head until his forehead rested beside it. Store-bought cookies. His world was upside-down.

Suddenly, he sat straight up. What a hypocrite he was. Christmas light battles. Calling hand-knit gifts a joke. Thinking that cookies decorated by his mother were lazy after raving about them for years. His own nephew thought that he was a failure because he couldn't wrap a gift as well as a professional. When had Christmas become about perfection? Jack used to know how to have fun during the holidays. Had his quest for perfect marketing material turned him into a snob?

No wonder he'd been having such problems with Christmastown. A person could create the perfect Christmas dinner. They could buy and wrap the perfect gift. But there was no way to control the chaos of spending a day at an outdoor park. Guests would be at the mercy of weather, of other families, and of kids trying to behave themselves in the face of rides and candy and meeting Santa. Perfect didn't stand a chance.

Jack needed to re-evaluate everything.

Starting with himself.

12. BELLE

"The worst he could say is no," Belle told herself as she pulled her toque lower over her ears. She was standing in her driveway, looking at Jack's house with hope in her heart. "Just do it. He won't say no."

She had a plan. Yes, they were at war, but she was going to ask for a temporary truce. There was a decorating battle to fight, and Jack Foster was the only man who could help her win it. Not for trophies or bragging rights, but for the spirit of the season. All she had to do was put one foot in front of the other.

Belle scurried over to Jack's front door and rang the bell before she lost her nerve.

He was dressed in a Christmas sweater, even though he was home alone. The reindeer's big red nose was centred in the middle of his stomach. She never imagined he'd wear anything so tacky; she didn't think he had a sense of humour. She kind of loved it.

"Belle?"

"Hi, Jack. I need your help," she said.

"What's wrong?"

"I tried, but I can't do it. I can't let Decker, Joy, and Charlie come home to an undecorated house. Joy texted and said the hospital would be releasing Emma on Saturday. I have two sets of Christmas lights that I didn't use. If we can run them along the eavestroughs, the house won't be totally naked for the holidays."

She'd hoped for a reluctant offer to help. She didn't expect Jack's immediate, enthusiastic, "Absolutely! Let me get dressed." He darted up the stairs and returned two minutes later. After he grabbed his ski jacket, Belle was surprised to see him put on his Secret Santa hat. Carolyn was right; it did look good with his coat. And the blue stripe complimented his eyes exactly as she'd thought it would.

"You said you have lights. How about a ladder?"

Belle shook her head. "I always borrow from the Hills."

"Mine broke when I was putting it away after doing the front of the house."

"It's not very late. The Hills are only down the street. I'll bet Tim will lend us his ladder again. It's for a good cause." she said.

"If your lights aren't enough, I still have Decker's spare keys from when I helped them move. He has two boxes of lights ready to go in his garage. It shouldn't take us long if we work together."

Belle's nylon snowpants swooshed as she hurried down the street. Tim wasn't home, but Amanda opened the garage and Madison offered to help carry the ladder. While Jack and Madison set it up, Belle unpackaged the

Christmas lights. "These have clips attached, so they'll slide right on to the eavestroughs. I don't suppose you have an extra extension cord, do you, Jack? All of mine are attached to my decorations."

The black-haired teenager raised her hand. "We have one," Madison said. "I'll be right back."

"Let's start without her. The outlet is around the corner. If we leave this plug end dangling, it should reach easily. Do you want to hold the ladder or climb it?" Jack asked.

"Hold."

"Okay. Let's do this."

The aluminum ladder clanked as they extended it until it stretched taller than the edge of the roof. They positioned it, Belle grabbed the sides firmly, and Jack began his ascent holding the string of lights.

The first two light bulbs took ages to attach to the metal eavestroughs. The next two went faster. Then they had to take a break to move the ladder. Jack climbed it again and attached six more.

"This is not going to be the twenty-minute job I thought it was," Belle said.

"And it's like working in an iceberg," Jack added.

"Do you want to quit?"

"Not on your life."

They kept moving in five foot sections. As they reached the end of the first string of lights, Madison returned with two extension cords. While Belle fumbled with frozen fingers to open the second set, Madison and Jack plugged in the first. Red, yellow, blue and green bulbs popped to life. They began at the upper crook of the drainpipe, and ran across the top of the garage door to the edge of the front porch.

"Come on, we're halfway done," Jack encouraged.

"I'm sorry, I can't stay. I have a test tomorrow," Madison said.

"You've done enough. We'll return the ladder when we're finished," Belle told her.

Madison ran off shouting words of good luck. Belle and Jack took a minute to untangle and lay out the next set of lights. Belle did her best to feed the string to Jack while holding the ladder steady. His progress was slow but steady. They worked foot by foot in the cold until Jack said the words Belle was longing to hear. "That's the last one. We're done!"

Belle rubbed her frozen nose. They stared at the house with its single row of lights. It wasn't much to look at. Still, it was *something*.

If it was her house, she'd add more. But Jack was a professional. He might think she was going overboard with decorations. Belle took a deep breath. For Joy, she'd put her idea out there and risk getting shot down. "I have a pair of lanterns at home that I used in my maze design last year. I'm not using them this time. Do you think they'd look good hanging from the flowerpot hooks on the posts of the front porch?" she asked nervously.

"I think that would work. I have some extra, big red bows at my place," Jack offered. "One on each?"

"See you back here in ten minutes."

Belle wouldn't be able to stay outside much longer. Her toes tingled in her boots. But hanging the lanterns would only take a couple of minutes. They'd give the house some character beyond the bare minimum of the lights.

"Belle! Belle Silver!"

She paused as the voice made its way through the

layers of her hat and hood. She spun around in the dark, looking for the source. Gord Dempsey stood on his front step, his ski jacket flapping open across his chest. "What are you and Jack up to?"

"We're decorating the house for Decker and Joy for when she's back from the hospital."

"That's awfully neighbourly of you. We can't help, but we've been watching you through the window. Clara has the kettle boiling for hot chocolate. You two come over when you're done for some hot cocoa and cookies. That'll be our part."

"We're almost finished. I'll tell Jack."

She hustled a little faster to get home, then wasted ten minutes trying to find the lanterns that she'd set aside when she decorated her living room. Eventually she found them in a bin in her spare room. "He's going to think I stood him up," Belle muttered to herself as she slipped her boots back on and trudged back down the street.

Jack was at the end of the driveway, stamping his feet. "You found them!"

Belle was taken aback at the lack of snark. She expected a comment about making him wait, or something about the quality of the lanterns when he saw them. Instead, he scooped one from her hands and bounded to the deck. He twisted some wire around the handle, and suddenly the nice but plain square lantern became a beribboned, eye-catching Christmas decoration. Jack stretched his long arm around one of the posts of the portico and tried to hang it from the hook that held hanging baskets in the summer.

It didn't fit.

"Leave it, Jack. It's too cold to fight with it." They

would both get frostbite if they stayed outside much longer.

The handle must have been too small, because Jack couldn't slip it over the hook. Then he pulled something from his pocket and snapped it onto the lantern. He tried one more time, and it slipped onto the hook like it had been made for it.

"What did you do?"

"I used one of the carabiners that was in Decker's garage. Come on, Belle. Let's get this done so we can get out of the cold."

She passed him the second lantern. "Gord and Clara Dempsey have been watching us from down the street like we're this evening's entertainment. Clara's making cocoa and Gord promised cookies."

"Then hurry up and hand over that lantern. Did he say what kind of cookies?"

Belle laughed, her breath making puffs of fog in the cold. "Don't worry, I'm sure she has more of her Bee's Knees."

When the second lantern was up, they carried the ladder to the end of the driveway and leaned it against a snowbank. Then they took a step back to admire their handiwork.

The house looked good. The lights and the bows announced to the world that the inhabitants were ready for Christmas. Belle didn't know what it was like inside, but Charlie could be assured that there was no way Santa would skip his house. It seemed like she and Jack were able to collaborate to produce a viable product for the holidays after all.

"What are you waiting for, Belle? Cookies await!"

"I need to say something." She took a breath. "Thanks, Jack."

"Thank you for asking me to help. We work well when we're on the same team," he said.

"I'm surprised at that too."

"Well, we both love Christmas. We're both competitive. And we both work hard. Maybe we have more in common than we thought," Jack said.

Belle considered his words. She never imagined she had anything in common with Jack, but he'd rattled off a list like it was nothing. Perhaps under his quest for perfection was a genuinely nice guy. She'd never had a chance to find out before this. She didn't know what to do with that. "Maybe," she agreed.

"Look at that. Another thing we have in common – we can change our minds about each other." He clapped his hands together before she could respond. "But that's enough deep contemplation for one night. Let's have some of Clara's cookies!"

CHAPTER 13

BELLE

Time was running out. Belle only had one day left to get her yard in order. She still hadn't come up with a way to secure her strings of lights to the hoops encircling the pole, or a way to raise the speaker so music would be coming from the tree itself. Even the two benches she'd placed along the edges of her dance square had started to tilt so that anybody brave enough to sit on them would slide into a snowdrift. Her decorating scheme was not progressing in line with her blueprints, but the results were in line with her other Christmas decorating attempts: bedlam and disaster.

Belle dropped the rope she'd unsuccessfully been trying to thread through a pulley. She needed a break. At least nobody was watching. As usual, most of the living room blinds on her street were drawn at this hour. A few homes had their curtains open to show off lit Christmas trees bedazzled with an array of decorations. The only witnesses to her failure were snowmen.

She didn't have time to worry about spies. At this rate, Jack was going to leave her in the dust. He had already hung all the snowflakes he wanted on his house, which was impressive enough. Then today in the cafeteria, she'd overheard him talking about his plan to add some to the evergreen in his front yard.

Belle groaned and gave up. The cord refused to fit through the pulley properly. She was stuck. That had been her last resort.

"Hello, neighbour. How goes the decorating?"

"Fine," Belle huffed.

"Still fighting with the zip-ties?"

"No, and this rope isn't working either. I think I'm out of ideas."

"Then it's a good thing that you have me next door," Jack said. "Wait there."

Belle had never considered her neighbour to be a good thing. She didn't wait because he told her to. She simply had nowhere else to go.

Jack returned from his trip to his garage holding a small box. "I can't stand it anymore. Try these," he said.

She opened the box to find a bunch of metal clips. "What are these?"

"The rest of the carabiners. I asked Decker about them, and he said I could have them since he wasn't using them. I thought they might come in useful. I can't use them, but I think that you can."

"Why are you helping me?" she asked suspiciously.

"Because I want to beat you fair and square. It wouldn't be a real victory if you couldn't have a complete entry." Then he added, "Besides, you've had that flagpole in the middle of your front yard forever, and you haven't even run up a Canadian flag as a placeholder. I need to know what you're planning." When Belle hesitated, he pushed ahead. "You obviously have a lot left to do. We're both running out of time."

"Fine. You can come over."

Jack waded through the knee-high snow and stepped cautiously over the piles of wires, lights, and hoops laying on the ground. "What is all of this, and what are you trying to do?"

"I'm trying to create a Christmas tree made entirely of string lights. I need to attach them all to these hoops at the right lengths. As you can see, the hoops get smaller at the top to form a cone. But I haven't found anything that will hold the strings in place."

"It looks good in theory. I think these will work. Which is the top hoop?" he asked.

Belle lifted it carefully. Strings of green and white lights came with it. She held it steady while Jack threaded a carabiner around two the strings and hooked it to the hoop. Then they repeated the move five more times. "Can you raise it enough so that we can work on the second hoop?" he asked.

"Before we do that, I need to attach the speaker to the upper one as well. Or at least, create a way to attach it later for the judging."

"Speaker?" he parroted.

"You can't rock around the Christmas tree if there's no music to rock to," Belle explained.

A look of confusion flashed across Jack's face. A second later, it was replaced with one of wonder. He looked around the cleared area on her front lawn and exclaimed, "It's a dance floor. You made a dance floor!"

She didn't know why he was surprised. She had never been the type to fill her yard with inflatables or other decorations. She'd seen some fun displays that had those things, but they weren't her style. Belle liked to fill her yard with people. Her decorations were going to be her neighbours; she'd planned a live, interactive theme that the judges themselves would have to participate in. "I sure did."

"Your snow maze got tons of visitors last year. I'm lucky the Light Spectacular isn't won by popular vote."

Belle liked to think that was what made her such dangerous competition. If a person saw a decorated house, they might comment on it, but the memory would fade as soon as another Christmas scene appeared before them. If they interacted with the decorations, it would result in a long-lasting memory that would be talked about, at least till the end of the season. Belle may not be great at decorating but, as she said, she was exceptional at Christmas. "Can you grab the set-up for the speaker? If we can get the connector in place, I'll just have to hook up the speaker on judging day."

Using a carabiner was much easier than fastening individual ties. Belle and Jack were finished in no time. She waved him away for safety's sake and quickly hoisted her tree to test the lights. For a brief minute, her yard was illuminated like a two-storey Christmas disco ball. Then she unplugged it, and the world went dark again.

She beamed. "It worked!"

"It's going to look great."

"I still have to prepare the rest of the ground-level stuff, but the tree is done. Thanks to you."

"You're welcome. But now it's my turn," Jack said. "Unfortunately, I'm really behind. I have a lot to do."

"A deal's a deal," Belle said gamely. Then she smirked at him. "Besides, it's not like you're going to have a chance at beating me anyway, but I want you to have a fair opportunity to lose."

Her display was unique, but as all the awards proved, Jack's designs could be on Christmas cards. His house was fully covered in snowflakes. Half the bulbs ranged across the blue spectrum, from baby blue LEDs to navy incandescent ones. The other half covered every imaginable shade of white, from the stark fire-white Edison-style bulbs to soft hazy angelic glows. As he arranged the snowflakes that he still had to hang on his front yard evergreen, Belle realized that Jack's plan was to have alternating blue and white swirls working their ways from the ground to the star at the top of the tree.

"I borrowed the Hills's ladder," Jack said. "Will you hold it again?"

"Of course." As Jack hung each snowflake on a bough and plugged it into the next, Belle handed him a new one. An hour later, they were both on the ground, fastening the last of his extension cords together.

"You should probably light it to make sure they'll all come on tomorrow," Belle suggested.

Jack pushed the final two plug ends together. The alternating lights looked exactly as she'd imagined they would. He'd done it again. Belle suddenly felt a sinking sensation in her gut that her uniqueness wasn't going to be enough to win the December Light Spectacular when she was competing against a house like his. Then she shook off the feeling, confident that she'd be able to identify and add any missing pieces to her display before the judges came by. "Not a minute too soon," Jack said. "I'm freezing."

"We still have to get the ladder back to the Hills," Belle said.

"You grab that end. I'll take this one."

Carrying a ladder was awkward at the best of times. Clunky boots and stepping over frozen ruts in the street was nowhere near the best of times, but they arrived at the Hills with both themselves and the ladder still intact. After leaning it beside the front door, Belle was ready to go home and dive into a pot of soup. She was debating between clam chowder and tomato when she ran into Jack, who had stopped dead at the foot of the Hills' driveway. "Have you heard anything from Joy?" he asked.

"She's still in Winnipeg. Little Emma is doing better but the doctors want to keep her for a couple more days." She sighed. "Joy is hanging in there. Ginger says that Joy has been texting non-stop about how excited Charlie is to have Santa see his new house."

"They'll be bringing home the best Christmas present ever," Jack said.

"That's true." As they headed home, Belle took a breath. "Thanks again for your help. I wish you luck with the judges," she said.

"Good luck?"

"Don't get picky, Jack."

CHAPTER 14

BELLE

WEDNESDAY, December 21 – Judging Day

At five o'clock, Belle and every other employee at North Pole Unlimited found themselves stuck in the parking lot as the entire company tried to rush home at the same time to put the final touches on their house displays. Although not everybody had registered for the December Light Spectacular, even casual yard decorators wanted to make a good impression as the judges toured December street by street.

Belle got home and immediately grabbed her shovel. The cold snap that had tried to turn December into an ice cube had finally broken. The slightly frigid temperatures that had taken its place arrived with snow clouds in its wake. Mother Nature was dusting December with a coat of newly fallen snow, leveling out yards trampled by children and dogs until they resembled the fresh, unspoiled scenes that holiday seasons usually brought to mind. It looked lovely but it meant that Belle needed to clear her dance floor again.

She didn't know precisely when the judges would arrive. Each year, they took different routes to ensure they drove past every house. The judges' convoy would arrive, led by Nick Klassen and his classic red pick-up chauffeuring the contest organizer, followed by two other cars, one for each of the other judges. All the vehicles would have their horns honking and hazard lights flashing as they trolled the streets and avenues looking for the very best light displays that December had to offer. They'd stop outside a registered display, gather on the sidewalk and whisper mysteriously to each other. Participants were welcome to talk to them about their decorations and explain their choices. Bribes of cookies and cocoa were also specifically not outlawed in the rules, mostly because it was impossible to turn them down. Once the judges had made all of their notes, they moved on to the next property.

Belle planned to disrupt all of that by throwing the biggest outdoor Rock Around the Christmas Tree party anyone had ever seen. Her specially curated play list was designed to get people dancing, and her strategically placed benches would give others somewhere to rest and chat with their neighbours.

She was shaking snow off her carefully coiled hoisting lines when the silver silence of the winter evening was interrupted by the whine of a leaf-blower. She looked across her property line and saw Jack aiming the fall yard tool at his evergreen, blowing snow off all the boughs to ensure that every point of every star was visible.

He disappeared into his back yard and quickly returned empty-handed. Jack crouched under his living room window, and then his house sprang to life. Belle stepped into the street to take in the entire tableau. She'd only caught a glimpse before. The full effect was breathtaking. Jack's variety of snowflake shapes and coloured lights brought to mind a house in a snow globe. The additional lights on the evergreen in his yard finished the design to perfection. Belle was certain that one more light would have ruined the effect, and one less would have left something lacking.

Her next-door-competitor had done it again.

But she wasn't competing with Jack Foster for the most perfect house. She was competing for the best Christmas decorations. Belle could only hope that the final element of her design—the people at the dance— added the extra something she needed to impress the judges.

Belle held her breath as she slowly raised the speaker and her light-tree. It went up without a single catch in any of the strands of Christmas lights. She fastened the ropes securely and then reached for the extension cord. "Please work," she muttered as she plugged it in.

Suddenly, a dozen strings of green lights glowed in the darkness, creating an ethereal tree that looked like it was made out of stars. The occasional green bulb she'd replace with white or red added just enough colour to give the impression it was a Christmas tree without detracting from the entire effect. "Wooah," she exclaimed.

Winter nights had always held their own enchantment for Belle. The cold never felt as bad as it did during the day, and the moon and star glow reflecting off the snow always ensured there was some form of light. Belle was certain that her tree captured all of that magic.

Then she turned the music on.

"Jingle Bell Rock" started piping through the speaker. The music drifted across the road, drawing the attention of the children building a last-minute snowman in their yard. "If you guys want to come over for a dance party, you're welcome if your parents say it's okay," Belle called.

"Cool! Thanks, Belle!"

The next person to stop was Madison, who was out walking Bucky. "Belle, I love it! You did a great job."

"Thank you. And please thank your parents again for loaning me your ladder. Come back for the party."

"I will."

Clara and Gord Dempsey were the first to test out her dance floor. Heavy winter boots meant their swing dancing was done at half-speed, but they still cut a snow rug. After the first two dances, the couple collapsed on one of Belle's benches, laughing.

"You've outdone yourself again, Belle," Gord said. "I enjoyed your maze last year, but this tops it. Who would have thought I'd enjoy fresh air and exercise in December?"

"Doctor Iverson will be glad to hear it," Clara joked. "Do you want one more dance before we head home?"

Various other neighbours came and went as the evening wore on. To her surprise, she discovered that Jack had come over to join the party when the Christmas Conga line almost knocked her over.

Jack stepped out of the line of dancers and steadied her before shuffling her to the side of the yard. "Are you okay?"

"I'm fine. Shouldn't you be at home?"

"I can run next door when the judges get here in case they have any questions. I don't want to miss the fun.

People always leave here in a great mood. I do like fun, you know."

She didn't know how to respond to that. Luckily, she didn't have time to. Belle excused herself to greet some people from other parts of December. Folks from all over were driving around to see all the houses listed on the town's contest website. Most stopped for a song or two. Belle gratefully received tons of compliments. But next door, Jack got all the silence and awe as people stood in mute appreciation of the scene.

When Nick Klassen appeared with Dr. Tinka Kovac and the other two judges, Belle pulled out the big guns. "Come on, everybody, I need you to hold hands around the tree!" she called to the dancers on site.

Once they formed a loose circle, she called up her secret weapon and, unexpectedly, the Whoville Christmas song started playing.

Dr. Kovac laughed so hard she fell into a snowdrift, which set off the other two judges. Belle couldn't have asked for a better response. That was a memory they'd all have forever. She hoped it was enough to beat the fairy-tale Christmas scene next door because she couldn't compare when it came to lights and design.

After a couple of songs, the festival chairwoman approached her. "Another unique theme, Belle. This was inspired. I hope you are planning to keep the music playing in the evenings until after Christmas break is over. People are having a wonderful time."

"I will, Tinka."

"Excellent. But we have to move on now. Fortunately, not too far this time."

Belle turned down the music slightly as the trio walked next door to get a close-up look at Jack's yard.

Their laughter died and smiles faded, only to be replaced with looks of slack-jawed awe at his snowy world.

Belle couldn't hear what they were saying, but she watched them whisper to each other with awestruck expressions. She kept her chin up. The judges liked what she had done. People were having fun dancing in her yard, which had been the point of her whole design. Even if she didn't get the trophy, it was still a win for her ego.

Besides, there was still a chance.

CHAPTER 15

JACK

THURSDAY, *December 22 – Announcement Day*

Jack had been the most popular person in the cafeteria at lunch. He didn't let it inflate his ego. It had nothing to do with his house decorations. Word had spread that Decker had texted him a picture of little Emma in the hospital's nursery. The tiny pink bundle was swaddled in a white blanket. She had no hair; all the picture showed was a scrunched-up face peeking from under a tiny blue knit cap.

It had taken Jack a long time to figure out what was bothering him about the photo, which surprised him since part of his job was recognizing details and coordinating items. The blue yarn in the baby's hat matched his toque: the one that replaced his old one after it was ruined in Joy's rush to the hospital. Since North said that Joy said that Belle had knit the baby hat, and Carolyn had told him that his Secret Santa had made an extra effort to buy that specific yarn, the math said that Belle Silver was his Secret Santa.

He hadn't realized his work nemesis had paid so much attention. He hadn't advertised the fact that he liked to try weird-flavoured candy, but she knew. His second gift, the generic hand warmers, arrived after he complained about his cold hands at Christmastown.

Then there was the hat. Belle had considered him knit-worthy, and he'd behaved like a jerk. Carolyn was Belle's best friend. No wonder she'd jumped to Belle's defense. He hoped everybody from his department had taken his chastisement to heart and hadn't repeated any of his rude remarks.

The worst part was that Jack knew that Belle was aware of what he thought of her other handicrafts. He'd laughed about her baking attempts at the bake sale. And he'd made comments about the painting she'd done and hung in her own home. It must have taken nerves of steel for her to send that hat through the interoffice mail knowing the reception it might receive.

He wanted to kick his own butt.

He needed to apologize, big time. Fortunately, he knew the perfect way to do it. The only question was whether or not Belle would give him the chance once the contest results were out. Aesthetically, Jack knew his light display knocked the socks off of Belle's tree; if the judges were marking solely on looks, he had the trophy in the bag. But if they gave points for fun and originality, Belle was going to leave him in the dust.

Jack spotted Belle on the other side of the community centre as the contest entrants and all the spectators that could fit crowded into the auditorium. Amanda Hill helped Dr. Kovac onto a square block, and she waved to get everyone's attention.

"The December Light Spectacular Decorating Contest had the most entries ever this year, with twenty-eight official sites. Our judges were busy last night, and we want to thank everybody for all the effort. Before we announce the winners, we would like to remind you that tomorrow night is the town tour, so you need to have your yards lit between six o'clock and ten o'clock for everyone doing drive-bys. The community centre will be open with a hot chocolate table and volunteers handing out maps with all the entries marked," Tinka began.

A few people clapped politely at the announcement. Jack held his for the real news.

"Now for what we are all here for. We had some wonderful displays this year. Our third place winner is the Mercado house with Flora and Ramon's Snowman choir!"

Jack had driven passed the corner lot. The Mercados had put together six snow-choir members and a choir director, complete with song books on stands, in front of a cedar hedge outlined with white lights. They'd done an amazing job giving each of the snow singers different looks and personalities.

"Our second place winner is the Phelps family with their animated light show. The committee isn't sure how you timed your lights to flash "Merry Xmas" and "Humbug", but we were certainly impressed that you managed to do it," Tinka continued.

Jack made a mental note to look into what he would need in order to do something similar in the future. It sounded like something he could use.

"And, finally, this year's December Light Spectacular

winner is Jack Foster and his Christmas Snow Globe! Jack, you did a beautiful job with all the snowflakes. It looks beautiful," Tinka said. "Come and get your trophy."

Jack spared a glance at Belle. She was gamely applauding like all the other entrants. He expected no less from her; she was always a good sport. After he and Dr. Kovac had their photo taken, he stepped forward. "Thank you to the committee members for volunteering your time to organize and judge the December Light Spectacular. I think December has more Christmas spirit than any other town ten times its size, and I'm honoured to be a part of it. I hope everybody has a chance to visit every house on the map, and when you get to Second Street, please stop by Belle Silver's Rocking Around the Christmas Tree display. Plan to stay for a dance or two. I tested her dance floor personally and promise you that it's a good time."

He watched Belle's eyes go big when he mentioned her name. Her face froze like she was uncertain to what he was going to say next, but he could see her brace for when the joke hit. When he went on to rave about her yard, she let loose the biggest smile he'd ever seen from her.

Dr. Kovac stepped back onto her box. "Thank you for coming, and we hope to see you all again tomorrow."

Jack was mobbed with well-wishers as soon as the meeting was officially over. By the time he'd spoken to everybody, Belle was long gone.

CHAPTER 16

JACK

Friday, December 23

Jack's hands sweated inside his mittens. He may have been making the biggest mistake in the history of Secret Santa. Not only was he deliberately revealing his identity, but he was also risking his very life to do so. Because Belle might kill him when she learned what he was proposing.

He hefted the grocery bag containing her last gift. It wasn't wrapped, and he had no idea if it would turn out to be a quality idea or a messy disaster. But that wasn't the point. The point was it was a homemade gift, made with friendly intentions, just like how she lived.

He figured that would win him some brownie points, if she gave him time to explain what he was doing. For his last Secret Santa gift, Jack had sent Belle a Christmas card with nothing attached. His anonymous note told her to be waiting at the foot of her driveway at five o'clock. At four fifty-eight he put on his coat. At four fifty-nine he opened his door.

Belle was pacing as she waited. Her unzipped jacket and bare hands fisted in her pockets said she didn't anticipate being outside for long. She was right, but she wasn't going back to her house either.

"Hi, Jack," she said in greeting. "I didn't realize that you'd gone back to add to Joy and Decker's house. It looks good."

"That wasn't me." He hadn't been back since they'd left, although somebody had. Not only were there the lights and lanterns he and Belle had put up, but now a trio of stars hung from the porch railings. Additionally, two rows of plastic candy canes stuck out of the snowbanks lining either side of the driveway. "I guess someone else had the same neighbourly thought that we did. Marking the edges of the driveway like that is helpful when you're parking in the dark."

"What are you talking about, Jack?"

"The plastic candy canes that somebody stuck in the snowbanks."

"I drove by their house ten minutes ago. There weren't any candy canes," Belle exclaimed.

Jack laughed. "At this rate, there could be a whole herd of reindeer on the front lawn by the time Decker and Joy get home. They won't be able to see the house for all the decorations."

"We have good neighbours," she agreed.

"Are you waiting for Santa?"

"Obviously. What else would have me outside at supper time the Friday before Christmas?" she joked.

He took a deep breath. "Ho! Ho! Ho!"

Belle's jaw dropped. "What? No!"

"Yes."

"You're my Secret Santa?"

"I am." He lifted the grocery bag. "I need you to come with me so I can give you your final present." She didn't move an inch. "Trust me a little bit. I think I've earned that much."

"This had better not be a joke, Jack."

"No jokes. Come on, Belle. I have everything set up at my house."

His Christmas décor was a lot different than hers. He had evergreen garland and lights wound through the banister leading to the second floor with strategically placed glittery gold bows holding it in place. The console table in the hallway held a red poinsettia and, above it, a seasonal painting on the wall showed a snowy pastoral scene with a horse-drawn sleigh in the background. The pre-lit tree in his front window had a precisely calculated number of red and gold ornaments to look fully decorated without being overcrowded. Jack tried to see it through Belle's eyes and decided she would think that he lived in a showroom.

Which was why, before he invited her over, he had Belle-ified his kitchen. He set a bowl of Mandarin oranges on his island, not perfectly centred on the marble. Then he'd dropped a handful of candy canes into a mug that he'd put on top of his usually spotless microwave. Finally, Jack had taped the Christmas cards that his nephews had sent him to the front of his fridge. He had to admit that the kitchen looked homier than any other room in his house.

"Come into the kitchen." He grabbed one of the two aprons he had laid on the island earlier.

"Is this a crack about my baking?"

"No! Not a crack. I know that you've had trouble in the past, but I wanted to share something that anybody can make because there's no cooking involved. My nephew Joey recently told me that my mother taught him how to make her chocolate-covered shortbread. I thought it was a complicated, seventeen-ingredient family recipe. It's not."

"I've had your mother's cookies, Jack. They're delicious. I could never make those."

Jack opened the grocery bag containing her present and pulled out two packages of storebought shortbread fingers and a bag of chocolate chips. "I'll bet you can."

Belle stared at him in undisguised confusion. "What?"

"These are all the ingredients for my mother's award winning chocolate-covered shortbread."

"Seriously?"

"I swear. I've rationed every batch she's ever sent me. I had no idea that I could have been making them myself for years!" he exclaimed. He didn't even have to wait for Christmas anymore. He could make them in April. Or August.

"And you think I can make these?" Belle asked.

"Can you use a microwave?" he countered.

"Yes, even I can't mess that up."

"Then we're set. You pour the chocolate chips into a bowl, and I'll open the cookies." But Belle stood, frozen. "What's wrong?" He didn't think he'd said anything to hurt her feelings.

"If we're going to bake Christmas cookies, we need Christmas music. It's an unwritten requirement to any recipe."

"If you don't have a dozen different holiday play lists on your phone, I'll give you every single cookie we make instead of splitting the batch with you," Jack said.

To his delight, she stuck out her tongue at him, obviously taking his teasing in the good humour that he intended. "Okay, so I have fourteen, but five of them are really short!"

"Call one up and let's get to work," Jack said.

He wondered if Belle realized that although he was giving her instructions, she was making the cookies all by herself. She melted the chocolate chips in the microwave, then carefully spooned the melted chocolate over half of each cookie before putting it on a sheet of parchment to cool and harden. She finished the first box in less than fifteen minutes.

He stood beside her as she contemplated the finished product. As far as he could tell, they were indistinguishable from the cookies his mom sent him every year. But there was only one way to be certain. "Are you ready for the taste test?" he asked.

"No. I probably scorched the chocolate chips in the microwave or something."

He mentally kicked himself for being one of the many people who caused Belle to doubt herself. "You'd have smelled it if you burned it. Go ahead." When she continued to hesitate, he reached around her, grabbed one, and stuffed the whole thing into his mouth.

"Oooh, mmmm," he moaned as the shortbread and chocolate crumbled together into a large bite of heaven.

"You don't have to pretend," Belle said as she nibbled a corner.

Then she groaned too. "So good!" she mumbled around a mouthful of cookie.

"Wait!" He'd forgotten an essential element of his mom's cookies. He reached into a cupboard and grabbed a pair of glasses. Seconds later, he filled them with milk and handed one to her. "We need to do it again with milk."

"If we must," she said with a grin.

Their second cookies with the milk were even tastier than the first. His third was enough to satisfy his sweet tooth. "Perfection," Jack said. "You did it."

"The question is whether or not I can do it again."

Jack pushed the shopping bag toward her. "You have enough to do two more batches. I don't know if you'll want to give them to your visitors or save them for yourself. Merry Christmas from your Secret Santa, Belle" he said.

"Thank you, Jack. Sincerely." She twisted the glass on the countertop, leaving a pattern of condensation rings on the marble. "I have to ask. What was with the keychain?"

"I was hoping you'd see the carabiner and be inspired to try to use it instead of zip-ties in the cold."

First, Belle snorted. Then she began laughing. "I totally would have done the same thing. Tried to help you without actually helping you, I mean. Thanks for that, even if I didn't win."

"People tend to stick to the traditional. That's something your designs will never be, Belle. You are full of fun and activity and celebrating with friends and family. It's another, very important facet of Christmas that a lot of people forget. Including me. It doesn't translate well to pictures, but I'll bet it's the reason that North put you on the Christmastown project. I'm the kind of person who makes mementos. You make memories. The world needs both of us."

Belle raised her glass of milk. "Imagine what we could do if we combined forces."

Jack laughed. "Christmas would never be the same."

Certainly not for him. He felt that he had taken off a set of perfect-vision glasses. Some things were going to get lost in the blur, but he could see everything else a lot more clearly.

Before he could say anything else, an alarm sounded on Belle's phone. Her shoulders dropped as she turned it off. "I'm sorry but I have to go. I have to start the music and get ready for the December Light Spectacular Grand Tour." She looked right at him, her brown eyes staring right into his blue ones. "I wish I didn't have to go."

"Do you need a hand running your dance floor? I have nothing else on tonight?" Jack didn't know where the offer to help came from. Maybe the fact that they'd spent an hour together and he'd had a better time than he ever imagined possible. "Our truce doesn't have to end after the holidays."

She gave him a smile he'd never seen before. "Maybe it doesn't."

CHAPTER 17

BELLE

"I see the car!" Belle hopped from foot to foot for two reasons. She was excited to get her first glimpse of Emma when Decker and Joy carried the newborn from the car to the house, even if all she got to see was a tiny nose sticking out from under a blanket. The second reason was that it was freezing again, and her toes were starting to tingle from the cold.

It was a small price to pay to see their faces when they saw their house.

The elves had struck again. Somebody had added a pair of badly misshapen snowmen on one side of the yard, while an inflatable dinosaur in a Santa hat stood guard on the front porch. Pots of evergreen boughs decorated with bright red ribbons and ornaments sat on each of the three steps leading to the sidewalk. There wasn't a space on the house that didn't have something in it. Folks were determined that their new neighbours were going to return to a house ready for Christmas and Belle couldn't be more proud of their efforts.

She, Jack, Clara and Gord Dempsey, and all the Hills lined up on the driveway. Belle saw Joy wave in greeting, but her attention was focused on the wide-eyed toddler in the rear car seat. Although the doors were closed, Belle swore she could hear the "Mom! Mom! Mom!" as Charlie took in his new, fully-Christmas-fied house.

Once Decker finished parking and had a chance to look around, his smile grew as big as his son's. He helped Charlie out of the car first and let him run around and explore the decorations. "What have you done?" Decker asked.

"We couldn't let you officially move in without marking the occasion. Besides, how would Santa know to stop at your house if it didn't have any Christmas lights on it?" Belle asked.

"Charlie has been worried sick about that," Decker said.

"Joy told us. We didn't do anything inside, so you still have the whole tree to decorate tonight, but consider the outside a welcome to the neighbourhood present," Jack told him.

Decker pulled Belle in for a quick hug and shook Jack's hand. "Thank you. I have to get the baby inside."

"We know. You don't think we're waiting in the cold to see you, do you?" Belle teased.

Emma was only visible for an instant. Belle got the impression of a well-wrapped little bundle with a scrunched red face wearing a familiar blue hat. It was enough. "Emma is beautiful," she said as she helped Joy out of the car.

"Happy and healthy and seven pounds. The good

news is, she has good lungs. The bad news is that she has really good lungs," Joy said. "She cried for most of the drive."

"Congratulations, you two," Clara said.

She and Gord gave Joy a quick hug, then headed home. The Hills did the same, leaving Belle and Jack alone with Joy. The red-haired woman looked at the two of them and said, "I can't believe you did all of this. How did you have time when you had to work on your own places for the December Light Spectacular?"

"We, uh, worked together," Jack said.

"You two?"

Belle's mouth fell open in mock outrage. "You don't have to sound so surprised. We're both adults. You were away, and we had a couple extra things laying around."

"And I still had the key to your garage that Decker gave me, so I knew you had already bought some lights that were ready to hang," Jack added.

"You two worked together," Joy repeated. "Without killing each other? Does that mean the Christmastown project is now on track when it comes to marketing?"

Jack made a see-saw motion with his hand. "We have come to an understanding on the concept. There may be discussions on execution."

"There will definitely be discussions on execution. Probably loud ones. But we both know we want to end up in the same place," Belle said. She had no expectation that her fragile new friendship with Jack was going to automatically make their work relationship all smooth sailing, but she didn't think they'd revert to their old enemy status either. Too much had changed.

Joy clapped her mittened hands together. "I'm so glad that my idea to send you two to Christmastown helped."

A thoughtful look crossed Jack's face, causing his blue eyes to crinkle. "That's right. North mentioned that it was your idea."

"And now you're working together outside of the office. I'm a genius!" Joy crowed.

"Stop gloating and have a cookie," Belle ordered. She peeled the lid from her plastic container.

"Are those Mrs. Foster's chocolate dipped shortbreads? I have been craving those!"

"They're her recipe," Belle hedged.

Joy ate one in two bites. "So good!" She grabbed another. "Jack, they're delicious."

"I didn't make them." Then the traitor pointed at Belle.

The cookie froze halfway to Joy's mouth.

"Jack taught me his family recipe. I'm sworn to secrecy." She wasn't about to let everybody know how easy the cookies were. They were something she could make and they'd be welcome to the party every time. And Jack knew it. He'd given her more than a simple recipe. He'd given her a way to succeed at the perfect Christmas cookie: something she'd never had before. That had been his real gift.

Joy chomped the second cookie in half, shoving both pieces into her mouth. Then she grabbed Belle's container. "Nope, I can't let you do it. These are terrible. I can't let them loose in the world." She grabbed a third cookie. "Wait? He gave you his family recipe?"

"It was my final Secret Santa gift to her," Jack admitted.

"I knew it would work!" Joy exclaimed.

"What? How could you know it would work if Secret Santas are drawn randomly?" Belle asked.

"Absolutely nothing. I had nothing to do with it. Charlie, it's time to go inside!" Joy shouted. "Thank you again for everything. I'll return the cookie container later. Gotta go!"

Joy left a swirl of snowflakes in her wake. Charlie abandoned his examination of the inflatable dinosaur when he saw that his mom had cookies. He followed her into the house, leaving Jack and Belle alone on the driveway. "Did we get played by a pregnant lady?" Jack asked.

"I know she spends lots of time with Jilly. So, it's possible," Belle admitted.

"Do you mind?"

"Not really." Especially since things between her and Jack had improved so much.

"Me neither."

This could be the end. If she wanted, Belle could say goodbye and she and Jack would go back to being ordinary coworkers, saying hello as they passed in the hallway. It felt like a horrible way to end a new Christmas relationship. "Do you think we could talk to Clara and get her recipe for Bee's Knees Squares?" she asked.

"Why don't we stick with chocolate dipped shortbread?" he suggested.

Her heart sank.

"We can try a new recipe next Christmas. We should practice this one again to make sure it's perfect. Maybe at your place this time? I'll bring the shortbread if you bring the chocolate chips," Jack continued.

"Us working together again? I like the sound of that," Belle said.

It was another Christmas miracle.

CHAPTER 18

JACK

Six months later...

They were yelling to each other from other ends of their respective yards. The June sun beat down on them mercilessly, making an already stressful afternoon that much more uncomfortable. Jack was sweating heavily as he swung his mallet, driving steel spikes into his lawn while Belle used a can of neon pink spray paint to mark boundaries on her property.

There would never be a better time.

"Did you hear me, Jack?" she shouted.

"The whole neighbourhood heard you, Belle. Quit shouting and come here for a minute."

In the past half year, they'd gone from thirty below to thirty above, frostbite to sunburns. He and Belle were having a rare weekend off before the grand opening of Christmastown, scheduled to open its doors at the beginning of July. He had won more arguments than he'd lost when it came to the marketing campaign for the new year-round Christmas destination. Unsurprisingly, the ones he lost were went he started focussing more on the idea of guests experiencing a perfect Christmas scene rather than visitors making perfectly imperfect Christmas memories with their families.

He was learning. Because of Belle.

Their Christmas baking and decorating sessions ran into the new year. Then, they helped each other dismantle their displays. A few days after that, Belle had invited him over for supper after they'd shovelled Gord and Clara's driveway after a particularly heavy snowfall. He learned that if Belle wasn't stressing herself out trying to bake specialties for the holidays, she was a very good chef.

After she'd taken the chance to cook for him, Jack could no longer deny there was something between them. He'd been attracted to her while they were feuding, although he managed to deny it to himself. Now that they were getting along, he couldn't pretend anymore. Any time he got to spend with her only led to him wanting to be with her even more.

He'd tried to ask her out for a Valentine's date, only to learn that he'd waited too long; Belle had booked a winter getaway with girlfriends to Mexico. Determined not to miss another chance, when his birthday came around in March, he threw a party for two: himself and Belle. Their first date was the best party he'd ever had.

They'd been inseparable since that day. They carpooled to work when their schedules coincided, which was most of the time. He barbecued at his place, Belle made the side dishes at hers, and they took turns eating in each other's backyards. They'd gone to the Red River Ex, the travelling summer carnival, twice while it was in Winnipeg.

Today they were taking the final step that would cross the line from merely dating to having a serious relationship: they were planning a joint yard display for the next December Light Spectacular.

The thing was, Jack couldn't let them do it without Belle knowing exactly where he stood.

She grabbed a handful of black hair and stuffed it under her ball cap. "What, Foster? I thought we wanted to be done before noon when it got really hot."

"I need to tell you something," Jack said.

"I'm listening."

"I'm in love with you."

"Oh."

He kept going. "I used to think that you were annoying when we fought. Your faith in yourself is unshakable. I was convinced I had to be perfect, all the time. I was jealous that everybody liked you, even when they were teasing you. You're wickedly smart, hilariously funny, and the way you live your life to the happiest every day makes me happy just to be near you. I love you, Belle."

She stepped closer and went up on her toes. Then she kissed him, lightly and sweetly, leaving him with a tingle on his lips. "Your sense of style and your sense of colour are both better than mine. You never have to do post-presentation edits on your proposals because of typos. And I'm jealous of the fact that the fire department doesn't stop by your house to do spot checks in December. Your perfect tendencies on our dates tend to make me perfectly happy, which makes you perfect for me. I love you too, Jack."

After that, he kissed her. He never could have imagined that his worst enemy would become his best friend and then the woman he was thinking of spending the rest of his life with.

But that's the way things seemed to work in December.

THE END

RECIPE: BEE'S KNEES SQUARES

Ingredients

1 cup butter or margarine
1/3 cup honey
1 teaspoon vanilla extract

1 1/2 cups all-purpose flour
1 1/2 cups quick oats (quick cooking rolled oats)
1/2 teaspoon salt
1 cup butterscotch chips

1/2 cup slivered or sliced almonds

2 tablespoons honey

Directions

Heat oven to 350 degrees F. Lightly grease 9 x 13 inch pan.

Beat butter, the first amount (1/3 cup) honey and vanilla in a large bowl until smooth.

Stir in flour, oats and salt. Add butterscotch chips.

Spread dough into the 9 x 13.

Sprinkle almonds over top and pat into dough to make them stick.

Brush with 2 tablespoons honey. You may need to warm the honey to thin it to make this glaze.

Bake 25 minutes until golden brown.

Cool completely before cutting into bars. Makes at least 48 pieces

Freezes well.

ALSO BY ELLE RUSH

SWEET CONTEMPORARY ROMANCE

North Pole Unlimited

Decker and Joy

Hollis and Ivy

Nick and Eve

Rudy and Kris

Ben and Jilly

Frank and Ginger

Noel and Merrily

Jack and Belle

Prequel - Christmas Tree Connection (part of the Christmas Kisses and Cookie Crumbs series.)

North Pole Unlimited Collections (also in paperback)

Collection 1 - Decker and Joy, Hollis and Ivy

Collection 2 - Nick and Eve, Rudy and Kris

Collection 3 - Ben and Jilly, Frank and Ginger

Collection 4 - Noel and Merrily, Jack and Belle

Holiday Beach (also in paperback)

Shamrocks and Surprises

Pumpkins and Promises

Tinsel and Teacups

Fireworks and Frenemies

Birthdays and Bachelors (e-book only)

Hopewell Millionaires

Doctor Millionaire

Fall a Million Times

A Million Love Notes

Royal Oak Ranch

The Cowboy and the Movie Star

The Cowboy and the Pastry Princess

The Cowboy and the Constable

The Cowgirl and the Duke (coming 2026)

Resort Romances

Cuban Moon

Mexican Sunsets

Dominican Stars

Mayan Midnights

Complete series 4-book box set

COOKBOOKS

Heartmade Collection

Brunch

Mains and Sides

Holiday Table

ABOUT THE AUTHOR

ELLE RUSH IS a sweet contemporary romance author from Winnipeg, Manitoba, Canada. When she's not travelling, she's hard at work writing books which are set all over the world. From Hollywood to the house next door, her heroes will make you sigh, and her heroines will make you laugh out loud.

Elle has a degree in Spanish and French, barely passed German, and is learning Italian. She flunked poetry in every language she ever studied. She also has mild addictions to tea, yarn, terrible sci-fi movies, and home renovation shows.

To keep up with news and upcoming releases, sign up for her newsletter at **www.ellerush.-com/newsletter**.

www.ingramcontent.com/pod-product-compliance
Lightning Source LLC
Chambersburg PA
CBHW051947220626
47052CB00004B/831

9 781998 825295